Sixteen can be Sweet

MAUD JOHNSON

No part of this publication may be reproduced in whole or in part, or stored in a retrieval system, or transmitted in any form or by any means, electronic, mechanical, photocopying, recording, or otherwise, without written permission of the publisher. For information regarding permission, write to Scholastic Inc., 730 Broadway, New York, NY 10003.

ISBN 0-590-32204-X

SCHOLASTIC BOOK SERVICES
New York Toronto London Auckland Sydney Tokyo

A Wildfire Book

Cover Photo by Owen Brown

ISBN: 0-590-32204-4

12 11 10 9 8 7 6 5 4 3 2 1   10   1 2 3 4 5/8

Printed in the U.S.A.   06

CHAPTER 1

My sixteenth birthday was supposed to be a wonderful event — and the day became a horror.

I thought that when I was sixteen I'd find a "real" job after school and during vacations, rather than baby-sitting and walking neighbors' dogs to earn extra spending money. Maybe, I thought hopefully, it would bring me more dates, and a tiny, inner voice always added with wanting wistfulness that after I was sixteen my figure might fill out to provide curves where they counted most. In spite of long, blonde hair and green eyes, I was never satisfied with the way I looked.

I crossed the days off on the calendar. Three months . . . two weeks . . . one more day . . . But nothing was as I anticipated. Nothing. Never in my wildest imagination could I have foreseen all that would happen from the day I became sixteen in the spring until school reopened in September.

My sixteenth birthday fell on the last Saturday in March, although instead of getting ready for the party that Kay, my stepmother, planned to mark the big occasion with, she and I were at the hospital, sitting on hard chairs in an antiseptic corridor outside the emergency room while we waited for the doctors to tell us if Dad would live or die. I was so frightened my stomach seemed to be jammed with hard little stones, and if I breathed deeply the air scalded my lungs. My hands and feet were icy cold.

Kay was terrified too. She didn't admit it, but I could tell. Her mouth was drawn and her skin was a gray color, as if she was a cardboard cutout instead of a real person. I'd never known her to be that silent for such a long time.

Dad won't die! He won't! I told myself desperately.

But I knew it could happen. Four years earlier my mother had died in an automobile accident, and I had not forgotten the agony of learning to live without her, of watching my normally fun-filled, smiling father sink into a dreadful depression that lasted for months. I had begun growing up in a hurry then, in the two years between being twelve and fourteen, when my father was often wrapped in silence.

Luckily, Dad met Kay Weatherford, fell in love with her, and married her. He was himself once more and I became part of a happy family again — until the morning of my sixteenth birthday when my father was driving through downtown Cincinnati where we lived. His business partner and close friend, Frank Dykes, an architect like Dad, was with him and they were returning from inspecting an office building under construction for which they had drawn the plans.

The police told Kay and me the accident wasn't Dad's fault. Several eyewitnesses saw my father brake for a red traffic light when an out-of-control car zoomed up from behind and never stopped, smashing into the rear of Dad's automobile and telescoping it against a concrete retaining wall. Frank was killed instantly, his neck broken. An ambulance carried Dad to the hospital, and Kay and I were notified that he was in the emergency operating room.

"What time is it now, Jenny?" Kay asked me. We had been at the hospital almost three hours, an eternity.

I looked at my watch. "Twenty to four," I said.

"Why is it taking so long? Why can't somebody let us know something?" She was thinking aloud, talking as much to herself as to me.

"You don't suppose Dad di — " I broke the

sentence off, unable to finish it. I could not utter the word *died*.

"Of course not, Jenny," she answered too quickly and put her cold fingers on my arm. "It shouldn't be much longer."

The double doors at the end of the corridor swung open and a man came toward us. He was short and heavyset, with black hair and tired eyes, his loose green trousers and collarless shirt the sort of clothing used in the operating room.

"I'm Dr. Carruthers," he said. "Mrs. West?"

Kay, nodding, got to her feet. I jumped up also.

"Do you have a report on my husband?" she asked.

"He's out of surgery and his condition seems to have stabilized. We had to remove his spleen. It had ruptured and was causing internal bleeding."

"Will he be all right?" Kay's voice was unnaturally hoarse.

"Barring complications, I think he should be. He has some other injuries. Four crushed ribs and his left arm is broken just above the wrist. His cuts are more or less minor with only one — on his left shoulder — needing stitches, and, for a miracle, his spine is intact. Mrs. West, he's under sedation and wouldn't recognize you even if visitors were allowed in the recovery room, which they aren't. Why don't you go home and get some rest? You'll be notified if there's a drastic change in his condition, and you can see your husband in the morning. He'll be able to speak to you then."

A feeling of relief washed over me. A little of the tension that had made my body stiff ebbed away now that I knew Dad would live.

The outside air was cold with the blustery March wind more wintry than springlike. Neither of us talked much on the ride home, Kay intent on her driving. I had forgotten it was my birthday until we reached our apartment and saw the party preparations.

Bowls of salted nuts were on the tables, and Kay had put candles everywhere because she knew I liked them. My records were in an untidy pile in the middle of the living-room rug. I'd been bringing them from my bedroom when the message came that Dad was hurt.

"I don't feel much like celebrating now," I murmured.

"Neither do I," she sighed. "Let's call the party off, Jenny. You can have one later when everything is back to normal."

"That suits me. I'm just — just wrung out. I don't even feel up to letting people know that the party is cancelled."

She put her arm around my shoulders. "I know, dear," she said gently. "What about telephoning Angie and explaining the circumstances? I'm sure she'll make the calls for you."

Angie Craig was my best friend. I dialed her number and when she answered I told her about Dad, my voice choking. It seemed strange to be on the verge of tears now that I knew my father would not die, when I'd been dry-eyed during the wait at the hospital.

"That's awful, Jenny," Angie said. "Sure, I'll let the crowd know. I've been wondering where you were all afternoon because I've got news and I called your number several times to tell you. We're moving to San Francisco."

"Moving?" The word rattled around on my tongue. "Leaving Cincinnati? Oh, Angie — "

"Dad will go next week. He's had a big job promotion. Mama and I are staying on here until school is out since it's so near the end of the term. I'll miss you something fierce, Jenny, but won't living in San Francisco be fabulous? All the places to see. And California is simply loaded with guys!"

I felt sick. The first of the year another good friend, Joanne Jackson, had moved to Texas when her father was transferred, and now Angie would be living on the West Coast. Even if we tried to keep in touch it would never be the same as seeing her every day at school and gabbing over the phone with her almost every night. I had plenty of acquaintances, but not another friend as close as she was or as Joanne had been, and I'd never had a steady boyfriend. Kay and Dad had each other, but I seemed doomed to loneliness.

After thanking Angie again for telling everyone the party was postponed, I returned the phone to its cradle, staring at it for a long minute. Finally, I made myself pick up the records and carry them to their usual spot in my room. I poured the nuts into a jar on the kitchen counter and began to remove the candles.

A reaction was setting in. I knew I should be so thankful to have Dad alive that nothing else ought to matter, but it wasn't that easy.

Some birthday, I thought forlornly. Who in the world was crazy enough to call it *sweet* sixteen?

CHAPTER 2

The math book was open in front of me but instead of studying for the next morning's exam, I smiled in the direction of the big red circle on the desk calendar in my bedroom. That circle marked the beginning of summer vacation just six days away, the time when my job would start. I couldn't wait.

The job seemed too good to be true. I would be working at a swimming pool, first in the girls' locker room; but as soon as I passed life-saving tests — which I planned to finish by mid-June — I could be out of doors in the pool area. It was difficult to cram for math and the other examinations with balmy May air coming in my window and the realization that in six days I'd be at the pool meeting new people and having fun as well as receiving a weekly pay check.

Looking forward to the job had been the one bright spot for me since the end of March.

It kept my thoughts away from the fact that Angie was moving and, more importantly, it helped me endure the situation at home. Things were *not* back to normal in our family since Dad's automobile accident on my birthday.

His broken bones and surgery healed beautifully, but not his emotions. Dad's personality was different. He was more moody and silent than he'd been following Mom's death, going for hours without speaking, his face expressionless. The one time Kay drove him downtown was a disaster, because he became so upset in traffic that she had to bring him home immediately. Later she went to his office for his drawing board, hoping if he became interested in making plans for a house or an office, he might snap out of his glumness. That hadn't happened. He would pick up a pencil or a sketching pad, hold it briefly, and then open his fingers, letting it drop without having put a line on paper.

My efforts to talk to him got nowhere. I felt as if I was addressing a marble statue. He stared at me without replying or giving a sign that he was listening.

I was concerned, but I tried to take comfort in remembering how he reacted after Mom's death and he had recovered from that. Losing a friend, even a close one, could not be as rough as losing your wife, I figured.

Kay was frantic about him, although I didn't realize how frantic until the May evening when I was studying for my math exam.

About ten that night she knocked on the door and came into my room, sitting down on the edge of the bed.

"Finished for the time being?" she asked.

"Do I ever hope so!" I gestured toward the closed textbook. "If I keep on going over and over the stuff, I'll probably get confused. I'm calling it quits."

"Then we can talk, Jenny?"

The way she spoke startled me. Kay and I talked a lot and it was one of the reasons I was glad my father married her. She was ten years younger than he was, twenty-nine when she became his wife two years before. I almost felt as if she was my older sister, and she told me from the beginning she loathed the term "stepmother."

"I won't try to take your mother's place," she said then. "I don't want you to think for a minute that because your dad plans to marry me he has less feeling for you or that he's stopped caring about your mother. People have expanding hearts, you know. There's always room in us for giving and receiving more love. I hope you and I will have great times together because I love Ed very much and I want to love you if you'll let me do it, Jenny."

For some unexplainable reason, that early conversation with Kay popped into my mind as she said, "Then we can talk?" She made it a question rather than a statement, and glancing at her I felt my throat muscles tighten. The frown lines creasing her forehead and the shadows under her eyes aged her, and I had never seen her appear more troubled except for the afternoon of the accident when she and I thought Dad was dying.

The flippant remark I started to give about it being odd to talk about talking froze in my mouth. Instead, I nodded.

"Jenny, the Dr. Spence who has been seeing Ed recently is a psychiatrist," she said. "I don't know if you knew this or not."

I hadn't known. "Are you trying to say Dad is crazy?" I burst out.

"*No*, Jenny! You mustn't think such a thing! But Ed is — is mentally sick, which is *not* the same thing as being 'crazy.' His moodiness and depression are lingering and lingering. Growing worse too. He won't eat and he can't sleep and he feels guilty about causing his wife's death and, now, the death of a friend."

"Dad wasn't even in the car when Mom was killed," I said quickly.

"That doesn't keep him from feeling guilt. He has shut all of this up within himself. I suppose he's mentally punishing himself and he must be suffering horribly. If I touch him he doesn't notice it and sometimes I don't think he's aware that you or I are in the room with him. Even when I kiss him, there's no response."

She paused, clasping and unclasping her hands. "You're practically an adult now, Jenny, so you can understand things that might not have made sense to you at the time your mother died. That day you were at a school friend's house and your mother asked Ed to go for you early since the weather was bad and it was beginning to sleet. But he was watching a football game on television and didn't budge.

"They had words. Not a real fuss, just a disagreement. But it still haunts him that their last conversation was unpleasant, that he didn't do as she asked. He wanted to wait until the game was over, which was another hour. She thought he should go at once as the streets were icing up, and when he wouldn't leave the TV set, she went alone."

Recalling that terrible afternoon four years earlier, I shuddered. I'd known Mom was coming for me when she had the wreck, but I hadn't realized she first asked Dad to pick me up. That day I'd been at Joanne Jackson's. Mrs. Jackson drove me home where Dad was waiting to tell me my mother was dead.

"Ed blamed himself then and still does," Kay said tersely. "As for this recent accident, I showed him the police report absolving him, and Dr. Spence asked one of the police investigators to repeat the fact to him, but it hasn't done any good. What I'm leading up to, Jenny, is that Dr. Spence thinks it would help Ed to get well if he was in different surroundings, that a complete change of scenery is worth trying."

"You mean — " I gave a horrified gasp, "that doctor is going to put Dad in a mental institution?"

"Not at all." She started to pace restlessly

around my room. "Dr. Spence feels Ed should be in a quiet setting where he won't be bothered with the pressures of the city. He thinks that the noise of traffic is always reminding Ed of the accidents. Dr. Spence feels Ed must try to solve his own problems at his own pace. Some people can talk troubles out, but Ed won't. Luckily, I've been able to locate a place for us to spend the summer."

"When will you and Dad leave? Where will you go?"

She stopped pacing to stand in front of me. "Not just your father and me, Jenny. The three of us are going to the coast of North Carolina."

"No way! My job — remember?" I jumped up. "It begins six days from today when school closes!"

"I'm sorry about the job because I know how much it means to you, but you'll have to cancel it. There will be other summer jobs in the future and — "

I would not let her finish. "I can't cancel it!" I said hotly. "You don't know what you're asking!"

"Your father's health is critical, Jenny. We have to follow the doctor's suggestions."

"Well, *I'm* not leaving here! Dad wouldn't know if I was with you and him or not, and besides, I'm sixteen now and perfectly capable of staying in this apartment by myself."

"Oh, Jenny — really!" She looked exasperated. "That's ridiculous and you know it as much as I do."

I had not expected her to agree. In fact, the suggestion just popped out and I was surprised to hear myself make it because living alone for three months wouldn't be much fun. I promptly came up with a more logical idea.

"I'll stay here in Cincinnati with friends," I told her. "I won't earn a lot but I'll pay part of my salary to them for room and board."

Before I finished she was shaking her head.

"That won't do, Jenny. To begin with, both Joanne and Angie will be gone and I don't know of any other friends you might stay with, but even if one of them was here and their parents agreed, you couldn't do it. Your father would worry about you and the last thing he needs is another emotional problem. I'll need you too. When we're in North Carolina, Ed shouldn't be left alone for a while and you and I can take turns staying with him."

"Nothing but nothing is going to get me out of Cincinnati this summer, Kay!" I barked. "That job is the most important thing in my life and I can't give it up!"

"More important than your father?"

My face had to be turning crimson because it suddenly felt hot. "I want Dad to get well," I mumbled. "You know I do. But — "

"You are coming with Ed and me." She spoke in a tone I'd never heard her use, a voice which implied, Do-it-my-way-and-shut-up. "I've rented a cottage on the North Carolina coast until September. Apparently it's a remote spot, which will be perfect for Ed, and it's on a beach which will be nice for you. Dr. Spence doesn't think we ought to make the trip by car, not with Ed's feelings about automobiles, so I've made reservations for the three of us to fly down the day after school closes and I've hired a driver to bring our station wagon. The North Carolina real estate man will meet us at the airport and take us to the cottage."

Kay had already made plane reservations. For three, no less. My needs and wants didn't matter to her. She had paid no attention to what I said about my job.

Seething inwardly, I gave her a hostile stare. Kay was throwing her weight around despite that pretty speech she'd made when she'd married Dad about wanting to be my friend and not planning to act like a stepmother. Some friend she was turning out to be, I thought darkly.

Using her normal tone again, her eyes focused on mine and she said, "Your father has done things for you all of your life and this is the first time you've ever been asked to make a sacrifice for him."

Pausing, she drew a long breath. "Did you know that some months after your mother died he turned down a fantastic business opportunity to draw plans for an office building in Mexico? He knew he would have to go back and forth for more than a year while it was under construction, and there weren't any living facilities at the building site area that he felt were right for a child. He didn't want to leave you here, not so soon after Charlotte's death. Someone else got that assignment when Ed said no to it."

I opened my lips and shut them without speaking, too shaken to say a word.

Whirling around as if she could not wait to get away from me, Kay left, closing the door to my room in silence as she went out. Her last statements were ringing in my ears. I'd had no inkling of the opening in Mexico that Dad rejected because of me, just as I had not realized he refused Mom's request to drive across the city for me the day she had the accident which ended her life. For the first time I could understand why it took my father such a long while to recover from Mom's death.

Yet, through all that time he took care of me. He had hired a live-in housekeeper so I wouldn't come home to an empty apartment after school, and there had never been a time when I couldn't go to him with my troubles and problems and take for granted he would listen. This was true even after he married Kay — until the accident on my sixteenth birthday. Nothing had been the same since then.

Anxiety began to gnaw at me, an aching sensation. If Dad needed me now . . . if *I* could help him return to normal. . . .

I could not stand to think of life without Dad, and if he wasn't himself, if he never stopped being withdrawn and silent, it would be almost as if he'd died. A chill swept over me although my bedroom was warm.

Suddenly, I wanted my father so much I hurt all over. I wanted him to be as he'd always been, smiling, teasing me, talking to me, loving me. Choking back resentment at the thought of giving up my job, I felt tears come into my eyes. I didn't want to resign that beautiful job before having a try at it, but if all the things Kay said about my father were correct, he might never recover unless the process was started soon.

The soft May breeze rattled the Venetian blinds on the window beside my desk and ruffled the top pages of the calendar, so that the red circle marking the final day of school was momentarily hidden. It dawned on me how ugly I had acted toward Kay. She was trying to help Dad. She wasn't deliberately setting out to ruin my plans, and I'd spoken to her so angrily.

I found her in the living room. Dad had gone to bed and she was alone. The television was off. Only one lamp was on and Kay stood in the middle of the shadowy room, her back toward me, her shoulders sagging. She had her fingertips pressed against her mouth and she wasn't doing anything, just standing there.

"Kay . . ." I said her name softly.

She turned. Her eyes looked enormous.

"Kay, I'm sorry. Dad's health does count more to me than working at the swimming pool. I — I guess I was — was very selfish a while ago."

She made a small crying sound and stretched out her hands to me. When I clasped mine around them it was like holding ice cubes.

"Jenny, we must help him to get well," she answered desperately. "*We must.*"

"Are you sure going away will do it?"

"I'm not sure of anything except that Ed is only forty-one and he's too young, too wonderful a man to spend the rest of his life this way. These last two years with him and with you have been so good. I never thought there was that sort of real happiness in the world and I want it again for all of us." Her voice broke. "Oh, Jenny, I hope Dr. Spence is right, that this change of scenery and going to a quiet place will work the magic Ed needs. If it doesn't . . ."

The sentence hung between us, unfinished. I was shaken, panicky.

Kay straightened her shoulders and I had the impression she did not want me to have a further glimpse of the turmoil she was suffering. "Thank you, Jenny," she said quietly. "Now, both of us should get some sleep. I have lots to do tomorrow and you want to be fresh for your math exam. Good night, Jenny dear."

She flicked off the lamp and started for the bedroom she shared with Dad. I headed for my room. Math was the least important matter on my mind at that moment.

CHAPTER 3

As Dad, Kay, and I stepped from the plane I found myself looking at land as flat as a tabletop. There wasn't a knoll or the suggestion of a hill in sight. Woods and cultivated fields bordered the runway of the airport that served the small North Carolina town, and the afternoon sun blazed overhead as we crossed the concrete apron to the terminal building. That tiny, almost deserted terminal made me think of a doll's house in comparison with the hubbub of activity at the busy Greater Cincinnati Airport we'd left.

"Heavens, it's hot here," Kay said.

"And this is only June," I replied. "Do you suppose it gets hotter in July and August?"

"Let's hope not. At least we'll have an ocean breeze at the cottage."

Dad, as usual since his accident, made no comment. I noticed how thin he was, how pale. His eyes held a bleak, lifeless look and

Kay had her hand on his arm, guiding his steps.

A gray-haired man with a pleasant smile came toward us. "The Wests?" His eyes moved from Dad to Kay to me. "I'm Curtis Hunt."

He was the North Carolina realtor who'd made arrangements for us to rent the beach property. Kay had told me he would meet us and drive us to our house, adding that he had also offered to buy a few groceries so we would have food on hand when we arrived.

Kay made the introductions, explaining that we'd brought only overnight bags on the plane as our luggage was coming in the car the following day. "Then we can shove off," Mr. Hunt said, pointing to an automobile parked behind the terminal. He and Kay chatted as she and Dad got into the back seat, which meant I sat up front.

I was lost in my own thoughts as we moved through the flat countryside. Somehow, I'd expected to see the ocean from the airport, and the uninteresting rural scenery with an occasional farmhouse amid fields and woods was a letdown. Perhaps anything except my job in Cincinnati would have been a letdown. Resigning had been hard, just as hard as telling Angie good-bye, and to add to everything else, I was physically tired from the final days of studying and taking exams.

"Young lady, have you ever been in this part of the United States before?" Mr. Hunt asked.

With a start I realized he was speaking to me. I murmured that I had not.

"You'll like it. Everybody does," he went on as if he was trying to sell a piece of real estate. "We Tar Heels are mighty proud of our coast and you're lucky to be in the Cooper cottage, especially after you folks contacted me so late in the season. As a rule these houses on Pamlico Sound are rented months in advance. This one just happened to be vacant at the last minute since the Coopers' nephew, who has used the place in the past, is going to Greece. He's a college professor. Teaches history and he's off to dig in some ancient ruins this summer."

I did not give a hoot about the Coopers or their college professor nephew, but the phrase "on Pamlico Sound" caught my attention.

"Do you mean where we're staying isn't on the Atlantic Ocean?" I asked.

"It's on Pamlico Sound. The ocean is past the Outer Banks."

From the back seat Kay said, "You mentioned a beach, Mr. Hunt."

"You will be on the beach, Mrs. West," he insisted. "But it's the beach by Pamlico Sound." He shot a sideways glance in my direction. "Young lady, you look pretty unhappy. Maybe you folks don't know how nice Pamlico Sound is."

"You're right," I muttered. "I don't know anything about it."

That started the geography lesson. Mr.

Hunt began to spout out facts the way a tour guide would have done. Pamlico Sound was sixty miles long and twenty-four miles wide at the longest and widest points, he said, adding that it was an indentation on the Carolina coast separated from the Atlantic by the narrow sand bars known as the Outer Banks and Cape Hatteras.

"There are three navigable inlets from the ocean into the Sound, which means Pamlico Sound is fed by tides from the Atlantic," he added, glancing at me again. "I gather you're not impressed, Jenny. I have a daughter about your age and I recognize the signs."

"I'm impressed," I mumbled, figuring the white lie was more polite than admitting the truth.

"You'll scarcely know the difference in the Sound beach and the Atlantic Ocean beach except that the waves on the Sound are smaller. Pamlico Sound is salty and there's plenty of sand."

When I remained silent, he tried a new approach. He seemed determined to convince me we were in Paradise.

"This is historic country," he said. "Roanoke Island where the Lost Colony settled and vanished is just down the coast and so is Kill Devil Hill where the Wright Brothers flew the first airplane."

That sounded more interesting. I'd always liked history and while Mr. Hunt was boring to listen to, I began to pay attention to what he was saying.

"Do you believe in ghosts, Jenny?" he went on. "If the answer is yes, you've come to the right place, because you may find a pirate's ghost looking over your shoulder while you're here. Back in the early eighteenth century, Blackbeard and a number of other pirates made this section their stomping ground. All the hidden coves along Pamlico Sound provided nooks for those sea robbers to bring their ships for careening."

Pirate stories had fascinated me from the first time I heard about the bold sea robbers who roamed the Atlantic coast during the time the United States was being settled. "Careening?" I repeated as the term was new. "What is 'careening'?"

"Ships have to be taken out of the water from time to time for repairs and to have the barnacles scraped off. The pirates were too smart to sail openly into port like legitimate captains would have done, so they used these inlets. They'd find a deserted cove, tie lines to the tall pine trees, and hoist the ships above the water, a maneuver they called 'careening.' "

I didn't know whether to believe him. "Are you kidding about Blackbeard, Mr. Hunt?" I asked. "Did he actually visit this area?"

"He didn't merely visit. He lived around here for a time. The story goes that he built a house in the little village of Bath for one of his wives, the last one — he had a dozen or more that he married and walked off from when he got tired of them. *Sailed off* from them might be a better way to describe it."

"Can we see the house?"

"It's gone now. Could have burned or rotted away in the two hundred and fifty-plus years since then. Or a storm may have destroyed it. This coastline is mighty changeable. During my own lifetime new inlets have been cut and some of the land swallowed up by the wind and water during hurricanes."

"Mr. Hunt." I tried to sound somewhat bored, but I found I was growing more interested. "Did Blackbeard bury any of his treasures near where we'll be staying?"

To my consternation, he threw his head back and roared with laughter as if I'd made the dumbest remark in the world.

"I suspect this entire coast has been dug up at one time or another by people hoping to find pirate loot and get rich in a hurry, Jenny." He continued to chuckle but apparently he realized I didn't enjoy being ridiculed because he added, "You just may be the lucky one, though. Not much of value has been discovered, but there always has to be a first time — only I wouldn't count on unearthing a chest of gold bars if I were you."

With barely a pause, he stopped addressing me and spoke to Kay. "Mrs. West, we're coming to Clayton's Store on your right. John Clayton sells gasoline and groceries. It's the nearest place to you for shopping."

The store was a cinder block building with

gas pumps in front and a flashing red neon sign which said, "Open."

"See the highway marker ahead?" Mr. Hunt continued to speak to Kay. "That shows the end of state road maintenance and from here to the water it's a private road owned by the Coopers, your landlords. The blacktop surface ends with the state maintenance but the sand is packed down and you shouldn't have any problem driving on it."

We passed the highway marker, the automobile tires throwing out a swirl of white sand as we left the pavement. The dirt road was narrower but just as flat, although it curved occasionally; and despite Mr. Hunt's comments, it did not impress me as being especially hard-packed. The landscape changed, the cultivated fields replaced by marshes where mammoth trees dripping with Spanish moss grew in brackish brown water. As the car moved on, those marshes gave way to thickets of low, green tree-shrubs jammed so densely along the edges of the road we seemed to be riding between two walls of glossy leaves.

"Mrs. West, that lane to your left leads to the Cooper house," he said.

I twisted sideways in an effort to get a glimpse of the house, but couldn't see anything down the turn-off except more of the tree-shrubs. We had not passed a person, a dwelling, or another car since Clayton's Store.

"How much further?" Kay asked.

"The Coopers are two miles from you by the road, but it's only about a mile and a half if you walk the distance on the beach. They're a fine old couple. Their phone is the nearest one to you in case of an emergency. Of course, I can arrange for a phone to be put in your cottage if you — "

"No thanks, Mr. Hunt," Kay interrupted him. "We came here for quiet and to get away from all the commotion of city life. No phone, no stereo, no TV. Jenny brought her transistor radio, but that's all. Otherwise, we'll spend our time communing with Nature."

Oh, brother! I thought, groaning silently, ready to scream. Not bringing our portable television set had seemed a poor plan to me when Kay first mentioned it in Cincinnati, and now that I knew what a lackluster spot she'd chosen for us to spend the summer, it seemed even more stupid on her part.

We drove through pine woods and veered slightly to the left as Mr. Hunt shifted his foot from the accelerator to the brake pedal and stopped.

"Here we are," he announced.

It literally was the end of the road. The pines were behind us, and in front was a house with low, rolling sand dunes on either side, the dunes dotted with scattered clumps of grass three to four feet tall. Ahead, a glistening white beach sloped smoothly about three hundred feet to intensely blue water which stretched to the far horizon. Pamlico

Sound did, indeed, appear as big as an ocean.

"Didn't I tell you that you'd have a beach?" Mr. Hunt sounded as triumphant as if he had created it by himself. "A private beach too. This entrance to the house from the road actually is the back door. The front faces the water."

The heat swooped down on us as we left the air-conditioned automobile, but a stiff wind was blowing off the water and the air had a salty tang, deliciously clean and fresh. Kay and Dad fell into step with Mr. Hunt while I tagged along in the rear, studying the cottage that would be our home for the next three months.

To me, the term "cottage" implied a small white house with a picket fence and red geraniums growing in window boxes. This place was anything but that. It was rustic in a rather attractive fashion, a one-story building made of planks placed vertically and weathered to a brownish color — later I learned they were cypress wood, which could withstand wind and salt. Only instead of being constructed on the ground, the house was set on wooden pilings some ten feet off the sand, putting the living area where a second floor would have been. Except for a storage shed at one end of the ground level, we could look under the house past the pilings to the beach and the water. A sturdy flight of wooden steps led to a covered stoop and the back door.

"It's a bird house for people," I murmured.

"This type of construction is to avoid being flooded in case of high tides," Dad said.

I caught my breath. Dad had actually volunteered a comment! Kay's head jerked as she looked toward my father. It was so seldom he said anything at all that the sound of his voice startled me and it must have affected her similarly. This was the architect part of him speaking through the fog of depression encompassing his brain, a reflex action on his part, I decided.

Immediately he became silent once more.

"Dad — " I began, not knowing what to say next although I wanted him to continue talking.

He didn't turn or glance at me. The moment was gone as he lapsed into his frightening silence again.

I bit down hard on my lower lip, hoping to hide my disappointment. Kay must have had the same sensation as her shoulders sagged.

We entered a surprisingly modern kitchen which opened into a combination living and dining room with sliding glass doors leading to the screened porch, which ran across the entire front of the cottage. One wall of the living room was taken up by a rock fireplace with bookshelves on either side, the mantel filled with pieces of driftwood in a variety of shapes and sizes. The furniture was bright and looked comfortable — a sofa upholstered in green and white striped sailcloth, an assortment of tables and lamps, some chairs with yellow cushions. There was patio furniture on the porch as well as an old-fashioned swing suspended from the ceiling.

"The two bedrooms and bath are on the other side," Mr. Hunt said. "Incidentally, there's an outside shower under the house. Good for rinsing off after you've had a swim. Plenty of beach chairs and umbrellas in the storage shed on the ground level, plus some shovels and rakes in case you want to manicure the sand. Also, there's a supply of firewood in the shed."

"Do you think it will be cold enough for us to want a fire?" Kay asked.

"Sometimes it happens in midsummer. You have the wood if you need it and that's the only heat in the cottage except the electric stove in the kitchen. The power has been turned on so you can have lights and cook. Hot water too, and there's ice in the trays in the refrigerator. I checked that yesterday when I brought your groceries out. One more thing," he paused, smiling. "Please don't pick the sea oats." He pointed to what I thought of as tall grass growing in clumps on the dunes. "I know they look nice in a vase in the house but you keep them where they are. They help stop erosion."

Kay and I nodded. Dad, I noticed, was standing in front of the hearth, his face blank once more, his eyes dull as if they were covered with a thin film. I wondered if he was thinking about the house and its construction, if the architect part of his brain was functioning as it had moments earlier. Or, were his thoughts somewhere else? On the two accidents, and my mother and Frank Dykes, who were dead? Was he hurting so much inside that he could not overcome his sorrow?

Kay thanked Mr. Hunt and we said good-bye. As the realtor drove away, the stillness in the living room was awesome. Mr. Hunt had been quite talkative and I found some of his conversation boring, but that was better than the silence without him. I couldn't have felt any more separated from the world if I'd been in outer space.

"Are you tired, Ed?" Kay asked Dad. "Would you like to have a nap?"

"Whatever you want," he replied tonelessly.

She turned to me, her voice artificially cheerful. "Jenny, didn't you say you were going to put your swimsuit in the overnight bag you brought on the plane? Why don't you try out the water. Ed and I will get some rest and then stroll around a bit."

It was a good suggestion and I changed in the bedroom that was to be mine. Like the other rooms in the cottage, it had dark walls although the furnishings were colorful. The bed and chest of drawers were painted white and there was a red braided rug on the floor to match the red trim on the white curtains.

Crossing the screened porch, I left the house by the front door, the warm sand squishing under my bare feet as I walked to the water's edge. Two noisy seagulls rose into the sky from one of the dunes, their hoarse squawks filling the air briefly before they disappeared to leave the only sound the low sigh of the wind and the faint lapping of the water against the shore. Apparently our cottage was situated on a shallow point of land, for in the other directions nothing was in view but more water, endless sand, and the tops of the pine trees showing over the roof. The trees formed the woods at the back where the road ended.

The silence bore down on me. I didn't feel peaceful, just frustrated. All of a sudden I was dying with homesickness.

If I were in Cincinnati I would have been at the pool, enjoying the first day on my job. I'd be meeting scads of people my age, making new girl friends to fill the void left by Joanne and Angie, meeting boys. Maybe one of the guys would have fallen for me in a hurry and would have wanted to date me. Maybe —

I caught myself, conscious of the lump in my throat. I wasn't in Cincinnati and that swimming pool job now belonged to some other girl. To some lucky, lucky girl whose name wasn't Jenny West. Three long, desolate months stretched out like three eternities until September. Blinking hard, I was determined not to cry for fear I'd be unable to stop the tears, but I had never felt so lonesome in my life.

CHAPTER 4

The castle was gorgeous, a rectangle of sand with round turrets at each corner, a pointed tower on top, and a moat with a miniature bridge fashioned from a four-inch sliver of driftwood. I sat back on my knees to gaze at my latest creation. A whole hour had been consumed in building the castle, in scooping up damp sand, molding it with my fingers, and dribbling water over the turrets and tower to firm them. That could be fun if you were with somebody, but it became dull quickly when you were alone.

I jumped up, took a flying leap, and landed with both feet squarely on top of the castle, deliberately smashing it to smithereens. Sand flew everywhere. For some unexplainable reason, destroying it gave me a vicious sense of relief.

I must be getting nuttier than a fruitcake, I

told myself. But after all, if I needed another sand castle I could build one. What else was there for me to do all day? In the one week since we left Cincinnati, I'd learned just how slowly time can move.

A corny rock song came from my transistor, a tune I doubted would ever hit the Top Twenty of favorites. That particular radio station was the only one I could receive, and the music, such as it was, made a change from the eternal silence on the beach.

Dad had spent the week in a chair on the porch, staring at nothing, unless Kay forced him to go for a walk with her. Twice she'd put on her bathing suit and insisted that he get into swim trunks, but while formerly he liked to swim, now he merely stood ankle deep in the water, his gaze fixed on the far horizon. Even when she splashed him playfully, an act which used to start a water fight between them, he continued to remain motionless, his arms folded across his chest or hanging at his sides, his facial expression as bleak as ever.

"How long does Dr. Spence think it will take for Dad to show improvement?" I asked Kay when we'd been at the beach three days.

"He didn't tell me. I — I supposed I hoped for an instant miracle, that ten minutes after we came here Ed would begin to talk and smile and — " She hushed abruptly, her lips trembling.

Kay was a commercial artist working for an

advertising agency, and she had taken an extended leave of absence from her office after Dad's accident. I was surprised that she didn't use the days for painting beach scenes, because she had brought her easel and art supplies to North Carolina, but she shook her head at my query about it.

"Perhaps I'll paint later," she sighed. "I simply can't be creative when I'm upset over Ed."

Kay made quick trips to Clayton's Store for supplies. I would have liked to go with her — to go anywhere — but the first time she started out and tried to take Dad and me, he became so tense at her effort to coax him into the station wagon that she went alone, asking me to remain with him at the cottage. I did and it was a new nightmare for me. Dad sat on the porch and stared at the Sound, or he stared at something. He seemed to be in a trance with his gaze fixed on the sky, or the horizon, or whatever lay in front of him. At first I attempted to force him to talk by asking him questions, but he never answered and I wondered if he knew I was with him. Kay never stayed away long but by the time she came home I was so frightened I was on the verge of tears.

One thing was obvious: there was no improvement in Dad's condition.

Not having a driver's license was another summer sacrifice I was making. I'd be able to take driving tests and get my license in the fall, but if I'd had it before we left for North Carolina, I could have made some of the trips to Clayton's Store.

Kay and I shared the housecleaning. She did most of the cooking while I tidied up after meals, and the rest of the time she sat near Dad and played solitaire. She must have played two dozen games during each twenty-four hours of our first week in the cottage.

One week . . . seven days. It was eleven weeks until fall. Thinking about it while I was on the beach at the end of the first week, I stared morosely at the ruins of my castle, kicking at the sand with my toes. I had an hour to dawdle away before dinner. The sun was still high and the breeze had died, leaving the beach uncommonly hot. Just to be doing something different, I trudged around the side of the cottage and into the pine woods at the end of the road. Having already walked up and down the beach many times, I knew there was nothing nearby except more sand dunes and the same view of Pamlico Sound we had from the screened porch.

The pine woods were shadowy and cool. If that small forest had been a park in the city it probably would cover less than a fourth of a block, I mused, wondering vaguely if my father's architectural instincts had rubbed off on me. Before he was hurt, Dad constantly measured things, sometimes aloud and at other times in his mind, estimating sizes and shapes. Now, I too was measuring.

The pines were tremendously tall with no low branches, the limbs tangled together at the tops. I discovered when I tried to guess the circumference of the trunks by putting my arms around one tree that my hands did not touch on the opposite side. The sandy soil beneath them was covered with a thick layer of brown pine needles and a sprinkling of cones which must have fallen the previous autumn.

Several white objects protruding through pine needles on the ground caught my attention. I went to the closest one, stooping for a better look, and realized it was a rounded stone slightly larger than a dinner plate in diameter. Another stone, the twin of the first, lay some three feet away, and beyond were several more, all nearly identical and in a straight line, each rock about three feet from the next one. Going deeper into the woods, I began to count the stones. There were fourteen, the line of rocks ending as unobtrusively as it started.

"Jenny!" Kay's voice rang out from the cottage. "We'll eat in fifteen minutes."

I headed for the house to take a shower and put on fresh clothes before dinner. Kay waited for me on the back steps, a pleading expression on her face.

"Jenny, please try to talk a little tonight while we're at the table," she said. "I can't continue doing it by myself and last night you scarcely said more than Ed."

For some reason, that irked me. "I don't have anything to talk about," I muttered in a voice edged with sarcasm. "Nothing interesting has happened here — or haven't you noticed?"

"You can try, Jenny. For your father's sake. Even if Ed doesn't join in the conversation, maybe something you or I say will ignite a spark in him."

I did not believe it would. Brushing past her without replying, I went to my room.

Kay had the knack of making food tempting. She had set three places on the porch table with a wooden bowl of fresh fruit serving as a centerpiece. The green salad offered a contrast in color to the cold sliced chicken and the vegetable casserole.

The sun was going down behind the cottage, out of our range of vision from the porch, which faced east. At first Kay chattered a lot, mentioning the rich blue of the pretwilight sky and asking how far it was across Pamlico Sound to the Outer Banks as if she did not recall what Mr. Hunt said on our arrival. Dad ate mechanically. I had the notion he might swallow ground glass without a complaint if it was put before him.

"Jenny — " As Kay spoke my name I lifted my head to face her. "This afternoon I saw you in the woods behind the cottage," she went on. "Did you find anything of interest there?"

Her eyes pleaded silently. *Please talk;*

please say something, she was telling me as plainly as if she had mouthed the words. We were finished with the meal and it dawned on me that despite her earlier request, I hadn't made one remark since we started eating.

"Oh — yes — uh — I — I did find something." Stammering, I searched my mind to think of a comment, remembering the stones. "Rocks. Not a pile of them, but fourteen and all about the same size. They're spread in a single line through the pine trees almost as if they were a footpath, only the tops are too high and rounded for stepping stones."

"There can't be any rocks here," Dad said.

"But I saw them!" I caught my breath. For a split second I had forgotten my father was not himself. He sounded normal and he had spoken to me as matter-of-factly as he might have done a year earlier, using what I always thought of as his "business voice." Glancing at Kay, I knew she was as surprised as I was. Then, she began to smile, her entire face glowing.

"You won't find many rocks along the coast in the south," Dad said. "That's not true in New England, but here, if there ever were any, nature ground them up during prehistoric times millions of years ago. That's why you have this fine grade of sand."

"I counted fourteen rocks, Dad," I managed in a quivery voice. "All of them look alike too. Whitish and with rounded tops."

"Why don't we take a look right now," Kay said. "If we wait, it will be too dark outside to see much."

The three of us trooped down the back steps and Kay's eyes met mine, relief and expectation in them. Dad walked more erectly than he had in some time as we crossed the expanse of sand and went into the woods.

"See?" I pointed to the nearest rock. "I didn't make it up."

"I didn't mean to say you weren't telling the truth, Jenny," he answered. "It's just that finding rocks here strikes me as odd." He knelt, digging his fingers into the pine straw and earth to lift out a rock, cradling it between his palms as he studied it from all sides. "I'll bet these rocks didn't originate here or arrange themselves in that line," he added.

"Why do you say that, Ed?" Kay asked.

"My elementary course in geology was a long time ago and I don't remember enough about it to judge the type of rocks these are, but . . ." He shrugged. Placing the rock on the sand where he'd found it, he stood up. Whatever he had been about to tell us was lost and the familiar blankness swept across his face. Without speaking, he started toward the cottage with his head lowered.

I looked frantically at Kay. The spurt of hope had vanished from her eyes and she sucked her breath in sharply.

At that instant a heavy weight seemed to crush down on me so that I felt as if I was on the verge of suffocating, terrified at the thought that my father might never be himself again. He might occasionally take part in a conversation, as he just had, but what if he never regained his former personality; if he never returned to being the warm, affectionate man with a keen intellect who encouraged me to do my best in school; if he was never again the man who joked with me, and dried my tears.

I did not want to think beyond those *ifs.* I had lost one parent through death and it was possible to lose my father in another way.

No one spoke as we entered the cottage. Dad took his usual chair on the porch with Kay near him. After washing the dishes, I went outside again but there was a land breeze and the mosquitoes were swarming so I returned to the living room and attempted to read. My thoughts were on my father instead of the printed paragraphs, though.

Bedtime was the start of a long, restless night. I would dream and wake up, plump the pillow and repeat all of it. When the first pink light finally showed in the eastern sky I was very much awake and I'd had enough of the bed.

Putting on jeans and a sweater, I tiptoed through the living room so as not to rouse Dad and Kay at such an early hour, crossed the porch, and went on the beach. The air was cool and a mist clung to the surface of the water, making Pamlico Sound a pale blue-gray with the horizon lost in the early morning haze. The mosquitoes had disappeared and night tides had swept the beach clean, washing away the remains of my shattered castle and leaving the sand unbelievably smooth.

I sat down and pulled my knees to my chin, hugging my ankles and wishing I could wipe away the last three months. I was still frightened about Dad, but in the dawn things did not seem quite as hopeless as they had during the dark. I realized I'd have to try harder to help him, and that meant cooperating with Kay. I'd apologize to her for not making more effort to talk and I vowed not to act glum no matter how down I felt. After all, the summer couldn't be any easier for her than I was finding it for myself.

Great streaks of apricot and lavender turned the sky into a mass of shimmering colors as the bright rim of the sun showed over the far edge of the water. The mist took on a rainbow of irridescent tints. A new day is a new opportunity, my mother used to tell me. I felt better, a little less tense. Stretching out full-length on the sand with one arm curled under my head, I closed my eyes, not planning to sleep but just to rest a minute. Fatigue and worry and the wakeful night must have been taking their toll because I felt relaxed ... drowsy ...

Something cold and damp brushed against my cheek to cause a whisper-light tickle.

Coming slowly back to consciousness, I reached out to push it away, and when my fingers touched warm fur my eyes flew open.

I must have been asleep more than an hour as the sun was well above the surface of the Sound and the mist had evaporated to leave the water glistening under a vivid blue sky. The cold nose nuzzling me and the warm fur belonged to a small black and white dog who was furiously wagging his tail. Without doubt, he was the ugliest, scraggliest dog I'd ever seen.

"So she's alive, Pit," a husky voice said.

The sound brought me completely awake. Other than Dad and Kay, I had not seen another human being since Mr. Hunt drove off after bringing us to the cottage.

But stooping beside me was a boy who looked to be about my age. He wore faded jeans and a gray sweatshirt, his light-brown hair framing a lean, handsome face. One of his hands rested on the dog's back and his eyes, which were focused on me, appeared to be the same shade of blue as Pamlico Sound. As my gaze met his, he smiled, his teeth flashing very white.

CHAPTER 5

I sat up suddenly. "Who are you?" I burst out.

"I was about to ask you that same question," he said. "My name is Keith Ericson. What's yours?"

"Jenny West. Do you live around here?"

"Sort of. I mean, I've been coming here for summers as far as I can remember. Have you been asleep on the beach all night? You're lucky the tide didn't soak you."

"Of course I haven't been outside all night! I'm staying there — " I pointed past the dunes to the cottage and for some reason felt an explanation was necessary. "This morning I got up early and came out of doors before sunrise. I must have dozed off without realizing it."

He looked doubtful. "Unc said the place was rented to a couple from Cincinnati."

"It is. To my family which means my parents and me. Who is 'Unc'?"

"Jonathan Cooper, my great uncle, my father's uncle. Unc owns this property and he never said a word about somebody like you — " Keith stopped, appearing embarrassed. "I didn't mean that as a slam. It's actually the opposite. I wasn't keen about coming here this summer but I didn't have much choice about it, only I never thought I'd discover a girl living just down the beach."

"Then we have something in common," I said and smiled. "I didn't want to come here, either."

"Why not?"

"I had a swimming pool job at home, but my father was hurt in an accident last spring and the doctors believe a quiet spot like this will help him." I took a long breath. "It's certainly quiet. Some days I've been scared I'd start talking to the seagulls. What about you?"

He sat down beside me, picking up a fistful of sand which he let run through his fingers. "It's not a big, earth-shaking tale."

"Try me."

It was easy to smile at him again. There was an open manner and a friendliness about Keith Ericson which made him as likeable as he was good looking. Also, my curiosity was aroused.

"Okay. It was a dark and stormy night . . . Isn't that the way all epics are supposed to start?"

I burst out laughing. "You can skip the weather report."

"Well, it's like this. My father feels responsible for Unc and Aunt Cammie, who is Unc's wife, because they raised him after his own parents died. They live in a small town in the central section of the state, but they've been coming here to the Sound every summer for ages. They built the cottage you're in as a gift for my dad and my mother, only my parents got a divorce. Mom's remarried and I live in Milwaukee with her and her husband in the winter and go to school there, but summers I've always come here with Jake."

"Jake?"

"My father. My real father, I mean. If the cottage is rented, he and I stay with Unc and Aunt Cammie."

"Your father gets a three-month vacation every summer?"

"He's a college professor in Pennsylvania. Teaches history. This summer, though, I hoped he and I might stay there in his apartment and I'd get a job until the end of August. My school opens the middle of September and so does Jake's college, so we'd still have had some time here at the beach." He found a piece of broken shell in the sand and hurled it far out into the water. "I like Pamlico Sound, and Unc and Aunt Cammie are the greatest, but to be honest, there's not much action around here. It gets darned boring to have three months without anyone my own age."

I understood. One week almost finished me. "Your dad wouldn't agree to what you wanted?" I asked.

"I didn't get around to discussing it with him." Keith gave a twisted smile. "Jake phoned me in April to say he'd been invited to go to the Greek Islands on an archaeological dig. He was dying to make the trip, except that he didn't like the idea of Unc and Aunt Cammie being here alone since both of them are in their late seventies. Aunt Cammie's eyesight is so poor she's given up driving and if Unc got sick or they had an emergency, they'd need another person. Jake said he'd have to turn down the dig in Greece unless I came here for the summer — so, here I am."

"I wish I'd known you were on this same beach," I murmured.

"I didn't get out of school until day before yesterday and I only arrived last night. This morning I decided to jog a mile before breakfast. Pit was ready for a romp too. Weren't you, fella?" Keith's last remark was addressed to the dog who must have known it was intended for him as he wagged his tail.

"Pit is a strange name," I said.

"It's short for 'Pitiful.' Unc found him wandering along the road four years ago and Pit couldn't have been more than a couple of months old at the time. Somebody dumped him to get rid of him, I guess. He was so thin and scrawny everyone who saw him would say, 'He's the most pitiful puppy I've ever seen,' and we began calling him 'Pitiful,' which eventually became plain 'Pit.' I grant you he's not much in the beauty department, but he's smart and likes people."

Pit licked Keith's hand and came to me. I rubbed his head and received a wag.

"You've passed his inspection so you must be okay, Jenny," Keith grinned. "Incidentally, Unc and Aunt Cammie would have been over to visit if Curtis Hunt hadn't told them your folks wanted to be left alone."

I made a quick decision. Company might help Dad and even if it didn't, I could not believe seeing two elderly people would harm him. A visit would do Kay good.

"Kay, my stepmother, told Mr. Hunt Dad needed to be away from civilization, but that doesn't mean complete isolation," I said. "She'll be glad to see the Coopers. Maybe Dad will talk or maybe he won't. Tell them not to be upset if he's silent, but please ask them to come."

"Will do." Keith glanced at his watch and got to his feet. "I didn't realize it's nearly eight o'clock. Aunt Cammie will be mad if I'm not on time for breakfast because she usually makes blueberry pancakes my first day since they're my favorites. I'd like to come back later in the morning, though. That is, if you don't mind and don't have some other plans."

If I didn't mind. It was all I could do not to jump up and down with excitement at the thought of his returning.

"I'll count on it," I said, smiling broadly.

47

"Good enough. Be seeing you."

He and Pit ran off, moving on the hard-packed sand along the water's edge. Where the shoreline curved Keith looked back over his shoulder and waved to me without breaking his stride. I waved too, watching until he and the dog were out of sight.

The tangy scent of bacon frying let me know my breakfast must be cooking and I walked up the dune toward the cottage. It wasn't until I reached the porch steps and called "Good Morning" to Kay who was in the kitchen that I realized I'd been humming a tune.

CHAPTER 6

The beach became fun for me instead of the bore it had been the first week, and Keith made the difference. I wasn't lonely any longer. He and I were together the greater part of each day and I'd never known anyone I liked better.

Kay liked him also, and while Dad continued wrapped in his own thoughts, it seemed to me my father's face occasionally showed more expression than it had earlier. Perhaps that was wishful thinking on my part. I remarked about it to Kay and she murmured, "I don't know, Jenny. I just don't know. If Ed would only volunteer a comment . . . or lose his temper . . . anything."

The Coopers came to see us and they were charming. I'm not sure what I expected. Rustic, primitive people content to let the twentieth century pass them by without realizing men had been to the moon or that a thrilling world lay beyond Pamlico Sound, I suppose. They weren't that way at all.

Unc was lanky and raw-boned with thick white hair and a gentle way of speaking. He had been a railroad engineer before he retired years earlier, starting out in the time of coal-burning locomotives stoked by hand and finally driving diesel engines.

Aunt Cammie barely reached his chest in height, a small, effervescent woman whose eyes sparkled behind heavy bifocals and whose face appeared to have been made of wrinkled parchment. She looked as if she should be in black taffeta with a dainty lace frill at the throat instead of the red slacks and plaid shirt she was wearing. Keith told me she had taught piano and played the organ in her church for years, "retiring" from both when her husband retired from the railroad.

"Jonathan's and my world revolves around Keith and Jake," she confided to Kay. "Not to have had any children of our own, we're blessed to have a wonderful nephew and great nephew."

Later during that first visit when I addressed her as Mrs. Cooper, she stopped me with a warm smile and the suggestion that I call them Unc and Aunt Cammie.

"Most of Keith's and Jake's friends do," she added.

As June became July Keith and I drifted into

a pleasant routine. We spent the mornings on the beach, dipping in and out of the Sound, building elaborate sand structures and talking, always talking. Pit chased the tiny sand crabs that were washed ashore and that usually buried themselves in mud before he could grab one, and we laughed at his antics. He would swim out a short distance, ride a wave to land and race up on the beach, shake vigorously to get the water out of his fur, and immediately return to the Sound to repeat the maneuver.

Sometimes we had rain squalls and occasionally there were storms with lightning and thunder, but the bad weather seldom lasted longer than a few hours. Afterward, the beach was delightful, the sand washed clean, and the air very fresh.

I went with Keith to the Coopers until I felt as much at home there as I did in our cottage. Their place was similar to ours, the house made of weathered cypress set on high pilings, the wide screened porch with its comfortable furniture and multitude of potted plants overlooking the water.

Most days Keith and I ate a sandwich lunch at whichever house we were near and kept out of the scorching midday sunshine until late afternoon. We'd play Scrabble or Monopoly or just talk or read with Pit snoozing in a shady corner. Unc and Aunt Cammie took naps after lunch, and Kay, who did not care much for any games but cards, played solitaire or read. If we were at our cottage, at first we asked Dad to join us and he invariably refused. After a time I stopped suggesting it.

I learned a lot about Keith during those early days, that he was seventeen, that steak and cheese were his favorite foods with brown sugar cookies running a close third, that he was interested in all sports. He enjoyed reading science fiction, he said, and he liked to make things with his hands.

"I'm keen on motors and machinery," he said. "Maybe I'll be a mechanical engineer."

"That's not for me. Too much math. And I'll tell you something else I couldn't do. I'd never make a doctor. I almost threw up in biology lab when we had to dissect a frog."

He laughed and I joined in. He was serious again quickly.

"What field do you want to go into when you finish school?" he asked.

"Something having to do with history. Either teach or do some sort of historical research. Maybe find work in a museum."

"You and Jake must think alike. He's a real history nut."

"I love it. Always have, especially American history. I'm not positive of the exact work I want to do, but it will have to have an historical angle."

One afternoon Keith asked about my mother and I told him of her death, not leaving out any of it and even mentioning Dad's sense of guilt regarding her accident. I'd never spoken so frankly before about that part of my life.

"I still miss Mom." My voice was wistful. "But if she had to die, I'm lucky Dad married Kay. She's super."

"You're right about that."

We were quiet for a short time. I broke the silence. "Keith, is it rough having divorced parents?"

"For some people, I guess. But it hasn't been too rough for me. My folks are swell. Anyway, I don't remember much else because I was three years old when Mom and Jake separated, and she remarried the year I was in the first grade. I'd hear the other kids at school call their fathers 'Dad' so I began calling my stepfather that and he acted pleased about it. He's an okay guy. So is Jake, a really okay guy, and to keep from getting my two fathers mixed up, Jake suggested that I use his first name. He and I are great friends. I hope you'll have the chance to meet him before the summer is over, Jenny."

"Has he remarried?"

Keith shook his head. "He dates but doesn't appear to be serious about it. One time I asked him if he was ever going to have another wife and he grinned at me and said if he did, I'd be among the first to know. I guess he's happy with his personal setup just as it is."

CHAPTER 7

On Aunt Cammie's birthday, which fell on the third Sunday in July, I was invited to the Coopers' for supper. Southern people, I learned from Keith, often referred to the evening meal by that term although in Cincinnati we called it dinner.

"I wish I had a gift for Aunt Cammie," I told Kay the morning before the birthday. "Something unusual and nice. Is anything available at Clayton's Store?"

"Not that I've noticed. Jenny, I could do a charcoal sketch of Mr. Cooper for you to give her if you want. With so little time before tomorrow, it wouldn't be a very detailed drawing, but he has an interesting face and I think I can do it without his posing."

I thanked her profusely. Kay had the talent for getting good likenesses on paper even when she relied on her memory, and the sketch of Unc's head and shoulders was good. She drew him wearing the baseball cap he used to shade his eyes from the sun and she managed to catch his familiar half-smile to perfection. I had an idea Aunt Cammie would be thrilled to have it, and she was, but another good result was that the sketch started Kay drawing and painting again.

Late Sunday afternoon when I left our cottage for the Coopers', Kay had set up her easel on the porch and was working with pastel chalks on a scene of the dunes with Pamlico Sound in the distance. Dad, I noticed, seemed to be watching her rather than staring blankly into space. I wondered if seeing her busy made him ever so slightly aware of his idleness or if her sketching jarred his memory. Before this last accident he and Kay often set up their drawing boards side by side at home on weekends, Dad working on plans for a house or a building, while Kay painted for her own pleasure or finished up a drawing for the advertising agency.

As I came out on the cottage porch I hoped Kay was aware that Dad's eyes were on her. She had to be, I decided silently. She and I clutched at any proverbial straws, real or imagined, which might indicate a change in him.

My father didn't speak to me but Kay remarked that it was nice to see me in something other than jeans or shorts. I had on a yellow linen skirt trimmed with white braid.

"Keith said birthdays are big stuff in his family," I murmured as if to justify it.

"You look lovely. That yellow is beautiful with your blond hair and the color sets off your tan." She drew a few lines with a blue chalk before exchanging it for a green one. "Keith will be surprised to see you in a skirt."

I wondered why my face felt warm. Later I was glad to have put on the dress because Aunt Cammie also was wearing one instead of the slacks she referred to as her "beach togs." She was in the living room knitting when I arrived and she immediately called Unc and Keith to admire the drawing. They came from the kitchen, each with a dish towel tucked into his belt as a makeshift apron.

"Jenny, these men won't allow me to lift a hand, not even to peep under the pan lids for tonight's meal," she said as she placed Kay's sketch on the mantel in an honored spot. "I haven't the slightest idea what the menu will be."

"Driftwood soup and stewed dune grass," Unc joked.

Not knowing what good cooks Keith and Unc were, I was amazed at the great meal of steak, fried potatoes, and vegetables and the dessert of homemade ice cream dished up from an old-fashioned freezer. Unc set the metal cannister of custard into the wooden freezer bucket, which he packed with ice and rock salt, and Keith turned the crank handle until it no longer moved.

Twilight changed to darkness and we sat around the table a long time after we finished eating. Unc and Aunt Cammie talked of their first years visiting Pamlico Sound half a century earlier and told amusing stories about Jake's and Keith's boyhoods. I insisted on helping with the dishes so Keith and I did them together, and when it was time for me to leave he walked me home.

The night was clear and balmy, the sky peppered with very bright stars. There was a pale crescent moon.

"Make a wish on the new moon and it'll come true," Keith said as we started out.

"All right. I wish — "

"Shhhhh, Jenny. If you tell what you're wishing it won't happen."

I didn't know what to wish for. I wanted Dad to be well again. That was most important. But I wanted something for myself: always to be as happy as I felt at that moment on the dark beach with Keith. It was as if no one else in the entire universe existed but us.

"Do you suppose I could have two wishes tonight rather than one?" I asked.

"I'll give you mine and then you'll have two. But if you use my wish I hope I'm part of it."

"You will be." My voice was so low I could barely hear myself.

He reached for my hand, holding it, his fingers closing around mine. My hand fit in his closely. A soft breeze blew off the water, ruffling my hair. I stole a sideways look at

Keith and his features were a blur in the dimness, but then I realized it was my vision that had blurred, that everything was momentarily misty to my eyes from the emotion surging through me.

"Jenny, do you date a lot in Cincinnati?" he asked.

I swallowed hard. Should I fib and deliberately let him think I was more popular than I actually was at home? Boys, I had observed ruefully at school, seldom spent much time with girls who were not beautiful or popular, and I failed to fall into either of those groups.

I couldn't lie, not to Keith. Something about him, some innate sincerity, which was as much a part of him as his tawny hair and his blue eyes, forced me to be truthful.

"I date some. A little," I answered. "Not — not a whole lot, though. I don't go steady or — or anything."

"I don't either."

"But I thought you'd know scads of girls!"

"What on earth makes you say that, Jenny?"

"I — I don't know," I stammered, not wanting to mention aloud that he was handsome and attractive and athletic in addition to being just plain nice, everything a girl liked. "Why don't you date — much?"

"After school I usually play ball or run track, and at night there's homework. Last winter I worked Saturdays at a car wash. I guess . . . until now . . . I never met a girl I went for enough to care about being with all the time."

Went for. Until now. All the time. The phrases were magical. My head started to spin at the full meaning of what he was saying.

We stopped walking. Keith did not loosen his grip on my hand and I didn't want him to. I was breathing as hard as if I was running. Keith was looking down at me and when I lifted my eyes I discovered he was staring at my mouth. I wanted him to kiss me, wanted it so much I thought I would explode if he didn't, and I wasn't sure how to show him.

I didn't have to show him anything.

He bent his head and his lips touched mine, very gently at first. I don't know when he stopped holding my hand but I was aware that both of his arms were around me and they felt wonderful. My hands went to the back of his neck and we clung together.

I was the one to step away. I had to move or die. Thunder had never sounded as loud to me as my own heartbeats and there was a roaring in my ears.

"I've wanted to kiss you for a long time, Jenny."

"Why didn't you? Before now, I mean?"

"I — I guess — I — I — " He drew a ragged breath. "Okay, if you honestly want to know, I was scared stiff you'd think I was making a pass at you and that you'd be angry and tell me to get lost."

"I'm not angry. I don't believe I could ever be mad at you." Reaching up to his face, I slid my fingertips tenderly across his mouth. We kissed again.

After a minute I said, "Keith, how long is 'a long time'?"

"You want to know when I started wanting to kiss you? Ever since that first day when I found you asleep on the beach. You don't know how appealing you looked lying there all curled up."

"And instead of doing it yourself, you let Pit give me a dog kiss." I giggled. "Want to know a secret? I like your kisses better."

He threw his head back and laughed. We began to walk once more, his arm around my waist in the starlit darkness, our shoulders touching. As we passed the final curve in the shoreline and circled the dune near the cottage, pinpoints of light from our windows came into view. Keith stopped suddenly.

"What's the matter?" I asked.

"It's too late for me to come in, Jenny. I'll take you all the way to your door, but why don't I kiss you good night now before we're any nearer your house in case your dad and Kay are on the porch?"

It was, I decided instantly, an excellent idea.

CHAPTER 8

The week after Aunt Cammie's birthday Keith received a long letter from Jake and read parts aloud to me.

The day was oppressively muggy, one of the rare times without a bit of a breeze, and even the water of Pamlico Sound felt steamy. By four in the afternoon the cottage was unbearable. Tired of playing Monopoly, we went outside, setting up a beach umbrella to provide a circle of shade.

Keith squinted at some small, puffy clouds gathering on the horizon and speculated that we might see rain before bedtime. I hoped he was right. If rain cleared the air, most of the suffocating humidity would vanish.

He remembered the letter and took the envelope from the hip pocket of his jeans. Jake's previous letters were brief, one or two paragraphs, Keith commented, while this one consisted of four pages filled with descriptions of the area he was visiting.

The Greek Islands sounded lovely with their gray-green olive trees and the colorful villages built on the sides of steep mountains, the flat-roofed houses looking as if they were stacked on top of each other. I could almost taste the luscious figs Jake wrote of picking, and he told of being invited to the home of a native family where he ate a dish of lamb and eggplant called *moussaka*, finishing the meal with *baklava*, which he said was pastry drenched with a sauce of honey, butter, and ground nuts.

"That letter makes me want to take a tour of Greece," I said.

"Me too." Keith folded the sheets of paper.

"I've always wanted to see that country, anyway. It's so full of history and I'd love to see Athens and some of those temples which are a thousand years old. Didn't your father mention the archaeological dig?"

"Not this time. There must be nothing new to report. Evidentally that part of Jake's summer isn't much of a success."

"Hasn't he found *anything*?"

"In the earlier letters Jake said he and the others on the dig had come across some broken pieces of pottery — shards, he calls them — but nothing old enough or rare enough to be valuable historically."

"That's a shame."

"They'd hoped to discover the ruins of an ancient town," he said.

Keith looked so glum I attempted to cheer him up. "The summer isn't over," I said. "Maybe they'll still find that town."

"Maybe. But time is getting short now. Jake is due back the middle of August."

The middle of August. I could barely believe July would be ending soon and August beginning. A seagull alighted on the sand near us and Pit, barking loudly, chased the bird. The dog never remembered that four legs are no match for two wings.

"Jake must be disappointed," I said. "I guess he feels like all those people who dug in this area of the North Carolina coast looking for pirate loot and wound up empty-handed. The day Mr. Hunt drove us from the airport to the cottage he talked about it and said none of Blackbeard's buried treasure has been unearthed."

"I wouldn't mind latching on to some of it," Keith grinned. "A chest of diamonds or a stack of gold bars for a starter. Oh, maybe you could toss in some emeralds and sapphires and a few rubies for color."

As I laughed, excitement rippled through me. "If nobody has found the treasure yet, what Blackbeard stole must be here! *We* could even look for it. I've read lots of stuff about pirates but I never thought I'd be in a spot where they camped, and sailed, and buried their riches."

"Wise up, Jenny. Who knows where to look?"

"We could at least make a beginning. Mr.

Hunt called this area 'the stomping ground' for a lot of pirates."

"It's too hot."

His attitude was exasperating. I jumped up, ready to go into action.

"We won't be any hotter looking than we are sitting here doing nothing but growling about the weather," I told him. "Surely you must have an idea of the logical place for us to begin digging. After all, you've been coming to this area for ages."

He did not move a muscle. After a full sixty seconds he yawned.

"I don't believe Blackbeard or any other pirate buried anything of value," he said in a lazy voice. "If they had, the treasures would have come to light before now."

"*But it hasn't happened!* That's the point I'm trying to make."

"Gosh, I'd hate to see you really get mad, Jenny. You're buzzing like a mosquito right now and we aren't even feuding. Or — are we?"

I ignored that crack. The treasure was uppermost in my mind, but along with it was the sensation of being very close to history. This was not just reading about events in a textbook. Keith and I were a part of things that had happened more than two centuries ago.

"What about those ruins in Greece?" I came back defensively, unwilling to let him change the subject. "Your father is searching for something there that's been buried hundreds of years. Maybe thousands. Why are you claiming Blackbeard's treasures won't be discovered when they've only been hidden since the early 1700's?"

"Unc told me people used to come to this area of the coast by the carloads, armed with all sorts of measuring instruments and old maps, hoping to get rich quick by finding Blackbeard's buried loot. Those characters would walk over fields where farmers had crops growing and some even tramped through yards and vegetable gardens. The landowners got so fed up with it they posted their property and asked the sheriff to arrest trespassers."

"You and I wouldn't be trespassing if we dug on the Coopers' property. Keith, please. Until now, I've only read about things like this, but now — "

"Jenny," he cut in with a gritty sigh, "I just don't think the pirates buried what they stole."

"For heaven's sake!" I exploded. "All my life I've read about pirates burying treasures! They would make a prisoner or a sailor dig the hole for the sea chest of money and jewelry, then kill the man to keep him from revealing where the chest was hidden. If you weren't so stubborn and pigheaded, you'd admit it's true!"

I'd come on very strong and the instant I closed my mouth I realized it. Embarrassed, I sat down again and Keith, his lips clamped shut, gazed into the distance, his eyes narrowing. The silence between us was awesome.

"I'm sorry," I mumbled. "I didn't intend sounding so — so angry."

"Forget it."

I waited for him to add another comment but he didn't.

"Keith, I don't mean to beat a dead horse," I said slowly, "but don't you believe those eighteenth-century pirates sailed into the the coves on Pamlico Sound to bury what they'd taken from merchant ships?"

He stretched his arms high over his head, flexing his wrists. "Sure, pirates came here. There are written documents to prove that. Letters and court records. Naval records. But as to their burying treasures — nope."

"What makes you think that?"

"I'll tell you what Jake says. Back in the seventeenth and eighteenth centuries people didn't live as long as they do today and that went double for pirates. If disease or infection didn't get a pirate, he was apt to be killed fighting or die in a storm. Or be hanged, if he was captured and brought to trial. Why should pirates save for the future when most of them didn't have any future and knew it?"

I wasn't sure if Keith expected an answer from me. Apparently not, for he continued.

"They stole plenty but Jake thinks they spent whatever they got their hands on," he said. "If a particular voyage netted a lot of loot, some of those pirates might stay ashore for a while. Until they were broke again. Blackbeard was like that. He'd stop off in the

Bahama Islands, which were a hangout for thieves, or he would sail through Ocracoke Inlet from the Atlantic, cross Pamlico Sound, and go up the Pamlico River to the town of Bath. He made friends with the Bath people by giving them presents — mostly items he'd stolen, I guess — and he had a house there. In fact," Keith laughed, "he is supposed to have wanted to marry the governor's daughter but she turned him down."

"You've got to be kidding!"

"I'm not."

I was skeptical. "How did a pirate meet the governor's daughter, much less know her well enough to propose to her?"

"Blackbeard and the governor were supposed to have been pals. You'll have to get all the facts from Jake when he comes." Using his finger, Keith drew the rough outline of a skull and crossbones on the sand. With one swish of his palm he smoothed it away and glanced at me. "You're still not convinced, are you?" he asked.

"Not quite. Everything you've told me makes sense and I'm not questioning Jake's knowledge of history. But if even one pirate buried money and jewels . . . whether that man was Blackbeard or not . . ."

"Darn it all, Jenny. You're like a turtle. Once you get your teeth into something you won't let it go."

"Maybe there's a clue to where the pirates buried treasures, only we don't recognize whatever it is as being a clue." I spoke as patiently as I could. "If some of the pirates buried their stolen stuff here — mind you, I said *if* — a marker of some sort would have been left to show the exact spot so they could find it again. That's common sense."

"More like wishful thinking, Jenny. You're daydreaming."

"Maybe a tree with carving on the trunk . . ."

"Come on, Jenny! Have a look around and tell me where you see any trees big enough or gnarled enough to be over three hundred years old."

"Don't keep putting me down. It wouldn't have to be a tree. It might be a big piece of stone or — " I broke the sentence off. "*Rocks!*" I said breathlessly. "*Those rocks in the pine woods at the back of the cottage!* They could be the marker because they're in a straight line and that line must point to something!"

The derisive look he threw in my direction would have melted steel. "Wrong again, Jenny. Those rocks — "

"Oh, no, I'm not wrong!" I snapped, interrupting him. "You are but you don't want to admit it!"

"Unc can tell you everything you'll ever need to know about those rocks behind your cottage. They are a type native to England and probably were used as ballast on a sailing ship coming here." His smile was so smug it made me sick. "When the rocks weren't needed any further for that purpose, they were left ashore. Don't act so doubting, Jenny. It was done all the time back then. In South Carolina some of the streets of Charleston were paved with ballast stones."

It seemed impossible to force him to understand and I bit my lower lip. The sun went under a cloud. Both of us glanced automatically at the sky and I realized the rain might come sooner than we first expected. Weather wasn't important at the moment. I was furious with Keith for brushing off everything I said, and I felt myself becoming more and more determined to prove I was right.

"I'm quoting Unc and Jake about the rocks originally being ballast," he went on. "If you still don't think this is how it — "

I wouldn't let him finish.

"Those rocks behind the cottage are in a straight line, Keith!" My voice was hoarse with tension. "Aren't you ignoring that angle? If the stones were dumped they wouldn't have been stretched out in a line with each one the same distance from the next, not unless there was a reason!"

He leapt up. "Okay, you've talked me into it," he said. "Let's dig."

CHAPTER 9

I was alive with excitement as we ran up the dunes to the open space under the cottage, Pit racing along with us. Going to the tool shed, Keith hoisted two shovels to his shoulder and we hurried toward the woods.

"Pick your spot, Jenny," he said as we reached the pine trees.

"You dig here. I'll go to the other end of the line." Taking one of the shovels from him, I was surprised at its weight, and rather than carrying it, I dragged it behind me, automatically counting the rocks as I passed each one. . . . Eleven . . . Twelve . . . Thirteen . . . Fourteen. I plunged my shovel through the ground cover of pine needles into the sand.

Lifting it out took a good bit of strength. I threw the load to my right and quickly refilled the shovel's scoop, working feverishly several minutes before pausing. Perspiration

70

dotted my temples and upper lip, and I could feel damp trickles inching between my shoulder blades. My back was beginning to ache from the constant stooping and straining. Digging, I decided, must require a different set of muscles from those involved in swimming or running.

I was not making any real progress. As fast as I lifted out a full shovel, loose sand slid forward into the hole, so that for all my effort there was only a shallow dent in the sand in front of me despite the growing pile to my right.

Perhaps I'm not doing it correctly, I thought, wiping my forehead with the back of one hand. After all, I had never shoveled anything before in my life except snow, and snow stayed where it was put until it melted. Straightening up, I looked at Keith to find out if he was having similar problems.

I couldn't believe what I saw. He had not begun to dig!

The sand and pine needles near him were undisturbed. His shovel was stuck upright into the earth and he stood next to it, his feet wide apart, one of his hands held against his mouth as if that would hide the merriment on his face. Suppressed laughter spilled from his eyes and while I stared at him he removed the hand from his chin, giving a loud laugh.

"You're something, Jenny," he spluttered once he had himself under control enough to speak. "You ought to win first prize in a determination contest. The way you attacked that sand with the shovel would make anybody think someone was hovering over you, waiting to hit you with a whip if you so much as took time to breathe."

"How about telling me what's funny so I can laugh too," I said thinly.

Still chuckling, Keith sauntered down the row of rocks toward me. I dropped my shovel. It barely made a sound when it landed but pine needles skittered in every direction.

"The truth," he paused, his impish smile growing wider, "is that I arranged those rocks in a line."

"You what?" I gasped.

"Yep. Little ol' me."

The frustration inside me intensified. He had become impossible.

"If this is your idea of fun and games, count me out!" I came back. "I don't know why you act as if it's all a big joke but I happen to be serious."

"It is a joke, Jenny. I did line the stones up. Honest."

My eyes were riveted to his face and I held them there until he glanced away first. His forehead looked a little pink. Maybe he was embarrassed. *Great*, I thought. *Great*.

"Those rocks used to be scattered over this piece of land behind the cottage and there were plenty more just like these fourteen," he said. "People here wanted some from time to time to build chimneys or outline their yards, so Unc gave the rocks away until only what you see were left."

He moved his tongue across his lips as if his mouth felt dry. I said absolutely nothing.

"The summer I was eleven or twelve, I got the idea of lining up the rocks with an equal distance between each one. I gathered them up and carried them into the pine woods because it was cooler in the shade, and in case you're interested, they are exactly forty inches apart. Or, they were. That's how I put them and it doesn't appear they've been disturbed — until now."

Still staring at him, I remained silent. I was seething.

"Jenny — " He seemed puzzled. "Are you just going to stand there? Aren't you going to say anything?"

"You could have told me all of this when we were on the beach. You could have spared me making a fool of myself."

"When we were on the beach you wouldn't let me get a word in."

"That's not true, Keith!"

"The hell it's not! Every time I tried to tell you about the rocks and the way they got lined up, you'd blabber on about pirates burying stuff they stole and how you knew plenty of plunder was stashed here."

"I do not blabber! You're insulting!"

"Oh, man! Look who's making waves about insults!" he snorted. "Jenny, you refused to believe me when I told you what Jake said about the reasons pirates spent their loot rather than save it. I figured the only way to shut you up and convince you would be to let you work up a sweat digging. Doing that convinced plenty of other treasure-seeking dummies over the years."

He was enjoying himself watching me suffer, deliberately setting out to make me look idiotic. It hurt to realize he considered me a dummy and that I was the target for his overwhelming ridicule.

This Keith was different from the Keith I'd been with since the end of my first week at the beach. This wasn't the same Keith who admitted tenderly on Aunt Cammie's birthday that he had been wanting to kiss me, and since that night had held me warmly. The Keith three feet away was having the time of his life at my expense.

In a second I was going to cry. I could feel the tears coming. My throat muscles were tight and my eyes burned.

Breaking down in front of him would make me seem more vulnerable, and I was determined not to add to his pleasure. Brushing past him, I ran toward the cottage, not stopping when he yelled my name twice.

"Jenny — wait!" he called again. I didn't pause or turn around.

By the time I reached the back steps, tears were rolling down my cheeks. Kay was in the kitchen but I ignored her, going to my room and closing the door, falling face down on the bed. I felt like such a fool. *Keith, how could you?* I thought furiously. *How could you?* I must have sobbed hard two or three minutes with my head pressed into the pillow before becoming quiet enough to breathe normally, but I didn't move. I couldn't . . . not yet.

Kay's voice roused me. She knocked and said, "Jenny, may I come in?"

"No. Go away."

"Keith is in the living room, Jenny. He wants to speak to you and he seems upset."

"I don't have anything to say to him. Not now or ever."

Her footsteps made a dull clatter as she left. Murmuring voices reached my ears from another part of the cottage although I couldn't catch any words. A door opened and shut, the hinge squeaking slightly.

Rolling over on the bed, I sat up and looked out of the window to Pamlico Sound. The sky was ominous, heavy gray clouds boiling overhead. In contrast to the previous stillness, the wind was blowing and small whitecaps dotted the surface of the water.

Keith was hurrying from the cottage toward the Sound with Pit at his heels. Surely he isn't planning to swim with a storm almost here, I thought, and wondered immediately why the idea put me into a panic. What Keith Ericson did was his business and it should not be my concern. Not anymore. Not after he had made me feel stupid and humiliated.

But I didn't want him to be hurt or to drown. As I watched, he took down the umbrella we'd used on the beach, hoisting it to his shoulder in the same way that he carried the two shovels. Was he doing this chore so I wouldn't have to bring the umbrella to the tool shed? For some unexplainable reason a fresh lump came into my throat as he started toward the cottage and disappeared from my range of vision.

Another few minutes passed. Kay's footsteps stopped outside my door a second time. "Jenny, I must come in," she said and turned the knob without waiting for my answer. "Ed wants you."

"You mean he asked for me?" I could scarcely grasp what she said.

"Yes. He seems perturbed and I don't know what's responsible but — Jenny, he told me to call you!"

Hope was bright in her face. As I started from the room, she remembered something else.

"Keith left a message for you," she added. "He wanted to get home before the rain and didn't feel he should stay here any longer, but he asked me to tell you he was sorry. He didn't say what he was sorry about, but he was really insistent that I tell you."

Without offering her an explanation, I went to my father who was pacing the length of the living room instead of sitting motionless in his chair. That stunned me. When I appeared he twisted around and I drew a sharp breath at the animation showing in his features. The listlessness Kay and I had learned to tolerate since his accident had been replaced by a frown, and although there had been many times in the past when I dreaded to see my father scowl as he began to talk to me, now it was a blessed change.

"Are you all right, Jenny?" he demanded.

"Yes. Of course. What's this all about, Dad?"

"Just what is the trouble between you and Ericson?"

The question caught me by surprise and my face felt hot.

"No trouble," I murmured and sat down because my knees were wobbly.

"I saw you and Keith going around the cottage toward the back this afternoon and I don't believe I've seen that before. The next thing I knew, you were in your room crying and Keith was in the kitchen begging Kay to coax you into coming out of your room. When the boy left here he acted as if the weight of the world was bearing down on him. He asked Kay several times to apologize to you."

Raindrops splashed against the window, quickly turning into a downpour. The storm had struck. If Dad noticed, he gave no indication. He barely paused.

"Jenny, you know I'm ready to help you if you need help and so is Kay. If what Keith did today to warrant that much remorse on his part is something serious, I want you to let me know. Boys his age can be carried away easily and if he — "

"Dad, you're wrong!" I burst out. "Keith and I wouldn't! What you're thinking about hasn't happened!"

The frown lines in his forehead deepened and his eyes continued to bore into me. I could not decide whether he believed me or not.

"Keith and I had an argument," I admitted. "That's all."

I had to make him understand, to stop Dad from blaming Keith for what hadn't happened. To stop him from blaming me too, although at the moment that didn't seem as important as clearing Keith. If my mind had not been whirling, I might have wondered why I was standing up for Keith, but I felt as if I was on a witness stand in court before a judge who had already convicted both of us.

Talking about the afternoon wasn't easy, but I started at the beginning and included everything, emphasizing how positive I'd been that pirate treasures were buried nearby. My voice choked when I reached the part about going into the woods, but I described my frantic digging and how I glanced up to find Keith beside himself with amusement. Drawing a deep breath, I finished with the story about how the rocks came to be in a long line.

"Keith seemed to think it was a big joke for

me to break my back digging," I finished bitterly. "I don't know how he could pull such a dirty trick. I'd never do that to him."

The corners of Dad's mouth turned up in a very faint smile. I gave a gasp. He had not smiled since before the accident — at least, not in my presence.

At the same moment, that smile was a fresh hurt. "I should have thought you'd be on my side," I said angrily. "I don't see anything funny."

"I am on your side," he answered, "but I must confess this stunt of Keith's strikes me as funny."

That was too much. Dad might claim he believed I had been treated unfairly, but my father always told me actions spoke louder than words, and now his smile stung me.

Maybe I misjudged him or maybe he realized how upset I was, for when he spoke again there was a gentleness in his tone. "Keith is probably just as upset over this as you are," he said. "There wasn't much happiness in him when he left here and I suspect he has learned that practical jokes aren't funny in the long run, especially not to the person who is the butt."

"I'll get back at him if it's the last thing I ever do!" The sentence came from between my clenched teeth.

"Wait, Jenny-girl." Dad used a pet name he'd had for me when I was in grade school. "Aren't you making a mountain out of a molehill? Your pride was hurt — that's all. You have to be a good sport. If you can laugh at yourself even if you've had a rough time or, in a case like what happened today, if you can refrain from hitting back at Keith, you'll be better off than if you act like a prima donna. After all, he tried to apologize and you wouldn't listen."

"Oh, you mean because Keith happens to be a boy he can do or say whatever he pleases no matter what? And being a girl, I'm supposed to smile and lap it up?" I asked sarcastically. "No way, Dad. Aren't you forgetting this is the twentieth century? That Victorian theory went out a long time ago."

"It has nothing to do with boy or girl. It has to do with being able to laugh at yourself sometimes . . . and to forgive someone who hurts you. Especially if he's aware he's hurt you. But it's up to you."

He went over to a chair near the window and sat down, his back to me. I parted my lips to speak and closed them again. Dad's advice made sense.

Keith had told me once when we were discussing our schools that his football coach drummed the importance of winning into the team and promptly emphasized how vital it was to learn to lose with grace. Hitting back might provide me with a moment of exhilaration, but it would hardly be worth bringing an end to Keith's and my relationship or making him feel worse than he apparently did. Keith knew I didn't like what he'd done and that was the important thing. And I knew he did feel sorry.

Kay called that dinner was ready. I could not think about food although I was eager for the discussion with Dad to come to a halt.

My father did not talk while we were at the dinner table, but neither did he sit staring absent-mindedly into the distance. The change in him was not spectacular, although small as it was, it made Kay sparkle. I knew she must have overheard Dad's and my discussion as the door to the kitchen was open.

This change in Dad pleased me just as it did Kay, but I doubt if I showed it outwardly the way she did because so many other problems were tumbling around in my mind.

My thoughts were on Keith. I longed to be with him, to explain why I'd been so furious and to attempt to prove my ability to be what Dad termed a good sport. The knot of fear in the bottom of my stomach was growing, fear that if I did not talk to Keith soon, nothing would be the same between us.

"I'm going to the Coopers'," I told Kay as she and I cleared the table. "I'll stack the dishes and wash them later."

"You mean you want to go there tonight?" She shook her head. "It's pouring, Jenny, and dark as pitch outside."

"Rain doesn't bother me. Anyway, I'll carry a flashlight."

"Don't be ridiculous. I don't care if this is an isolated beach, you're not going to run around alone at night. Especially not tonight. With this much rain there's bound to be an unusually high tide with water pooling on the beach. You're a good swimmer but you could drown if you stepped into one of those pools and got caught in the undertow."

"I'll take the road instead of walking on the beach. I really do need to see Kei — "

"No, Jenny." Dad's voice came from the living room. "You can see him tomorrow."

I didn't surrender. This was too vital.

"Since you two don't approve of my going alone at night, will one of you walk with me?" I persisted. "Or drive me?"

"That's enough, Jenny," Dad said.

If only I had slipped out and simply gone to the Cooper house rather than mentioning my plans aloud, I thought miserably. If only I could drive . . . If we had a telephone . . .

Pouring detergent into the sink, I turned on the hot water faucet and began on the glasses, reflecting to myself with grimness that being sixteen years old had not changed my status or given my family new confidence in me. So far as Dad and Kay were concerned, I had not progressed past kindergarten.

"I have an idea Keith will show up here in a little while," Kay said as if she was reading my mind. "He must be as anxious to make peace with you as you are to see him."

Her observation had a cheering effect and I hurried to finish the dishes and get ready for him. After taking a shower, I put on white shorts and a blue and white striped blouse which Keith once mentioned liking. My reflection in the mirror was proof that the bitterness had gone from my face and I smiled as I brushed my hair and sprayed on cologne.

I went into the living room to wait for him. I wanted him to understand when he arrived that I'd always been what he called a "history nut" and that I was caught up not only in the idea of discovering a hidden chest, but in actually touching something people hundreds of years ago had. I wanted him to know me and what was important to me.

The rain slackened. I knew I wouldn't have much longer to wait.

Keith did not come.

CHAPTER 10

The dawn was so misty it reminded me of the other time I tiptoed from our cottage at daybreak with my mind in turmoil. We had been at the beach a week then and I'd fallen asleep on the sand, to be awakened by Pit's cold nose.

I headed for the Cooper house, thankful that in daylight I would not need to ask permission to go.

It was early, a few minutes past 5 A.M., and I had been awake since the first pale gray light showed in the eastern sky. The storm clouds were gone and the morning promised to be fair. When Keith came out around six o'clock to start his daily jogging, I wanted to be there. I planned to invite him to come home with me for breakfast, not daring to wonder what I would do if he refused. Part of me would die if he turned his back and said, "I detest people who can't take a joke, Jenny.

In the future you keep to your section of the beach and don't bother me."

The night had seemed endless. It was an ordeal to sit in the living room with Dad and Kay, waiting, hoping Keith would arrive and realizing as time passed that it was not going to happen. My father did not speak after his refusal to let me leave the cottage during the storm. His eyes were hooded and he appeared preoccupied, retreating into his familiar silent shell. Kay sat next to him and played solitaire until I marveled that she could endure shuffling the cards one more time. An open magazine lay on my lap but I made no attempt to read.

Things were worse after I went to bed. Eerie noises filled the cottage. The wind-driven rain pounded on the roof and the windows rattled. Sometimes the walls creaked. Loneliness made me tense, that special gnawing loneliness which only one person could remedy — Keith. I would not cry for fear I'd never be able to stop, missing Keith's good-night kiss, missing the warm feel of his hand on mine. Most of all, I missed knowing everything was right between us and having the assurance he and I would be together the next day.

Instead of sleeping straight through the night as I did normally, I must have awakened half a dozen times. Once I got out of bed and went to the window. The downpour of rain had changed into a drizzle, but the wind remained strong and Pamlico Sound was black, foaming with angry waves which rolled high on the beach. I admitted to myself a little grudgingly that it would have been stupid for me — or anyone — to be out in such a bad storm, but I made up my mind to go to Keith as soon as it was day.

At a quarter to five I awoke again. Enough muted, pearly light came through the window for me to see across the bedroom. Putting on jeans and a sweater, I moved silently through the cottage and down the porch steps.

Evidence of the intensity of the storm showed everywhere. Pieces of driftwood had been washed ashore, and the damp, packed sand of the tidal area extended well past the usual water line. The air felt cool without any trace of the previous afternoon's humidity. In the early light Pamlico Sound was the color of pewter, a color I knew would change when the sun came up, and tinges of pink and coral already streaked across the eastern sky.

I walked swiftly, my mind on Keith. We'd make a special breakfast together — if he still wanted anything to do with me. Pushing that fear away, I tried not to think about the possibility. He loved bacon and cheese omelets. Maybe I'd bake muffins. Kay had an easy recipe and —

An unfamiliar murmuring noise startled me, breaking into my thoughts. I stopped walking, catching my breath. For a moment I thought I heard a human voice.

My imagination had to be playing tricks. I was about halfway from our cottage to the

Coopers' and I could look along the coastline at the water's edge in either direction without seeing a soul. Pamlico Sound lay to my right and on the left were the low, rolling dunes dotted with a few clumps of sea oats and an occasional scrubby bush stunted by the wind.

Walking once more, I consciously listened, hearing nothing but the lapping of small waves. Ahead of me was the dune that Keith and I laughingly named "Big 'Un," since instead of lying parallel to the shore as the other dunes did, it jutted at right angles, dwindling to nothing as it formed a partial barricade across the beach, ending about a hundred feet from the water. When I approached, a flock of gulls flew into the air from the far side of Big 'Un, their wings moving wildly when they passed over my head.

The noise I'd heard came from the birds. They probably were roosting. Perhaps, I thought and giggled, gulls cooed when they first got up in the morning instead of giving their customary raucous cries. After all, some people sang in the shower, never uttering a bit of music at any other time.

To avoid having to climb over Big 'Un, I swung to the right, glancing toward the water where the scarlet rim of the sun showed over the horizon. The sky and the Sound were rosy. I circled the dune — and froze in my tracks.

Two men stood close to a small sailboat, which rested on its side.

They had been sheltered from my view by

Big 'Un until that instant. Both men appeared to be in their twenties, both in swimming trunks, the shorter one also wearing a zipped-up windbreaker. The tall man had wrapped a boat sail over his bare shoulders as protection from the chilly air.

My first reaction was complete astonishment. I think I gasped as I managed a "Hi." They acted surprised to see me and it was obvious they were pleased because they ran toward me, waving and shouting.

"At least we're not on a deserted island," the shorter man said and grinned. "It's damn good to know there's another live human being on this beach, especially when she's a girl."

"Oh, man, do I ever believe in fairy godmothers or guardian angels or whatever!" the other man spoke up. He had a great deal of shaggy black hair and a reddish complexion. "You don't happen to be carrying any food, do you?"

"No, I don't" I replied. "Where did you two come from?"

"You tell her how it is." The short man jerked his head at his companion. "You were the so-called navigator who got us into this mess."

They were vacationing on the Outer Banks across the Sound and had rented the sailboat for a day's outing, the tall one explained.

"At first everything was okay," he went on. "We'd brought along plenty of booze so we didn't mind the wind dying or our boat getting becalmed. But the storm hit and it was hell from then on. I didn't think we'd ever see land again. We were tossed about like crazy in eight-foot waves with the wind blowing us away from where we wanted to go."

"It must have been eight or nine o'clock last night when we hit here." His friend took up the story. "You can bet we were glad to get our feet on solid ground too. We beached the boat and got under it to sleep, but from the looks of the scenery this morning we're on a sandbar or an island. We just woke up and haven't had a chance to scout around."

"This is the mainland," I said.

"Any towns near?"

"No. There's a store, Clayton's, seven or eight miles away."

"You live here? You sure don't talk like a Carolinian."

"I'm spending the summer," I told him.

"Where? You got a trailer or a camper? Look, if you have anything with wheels, we'll make it worth your while to drive us to the Outer Banks no matter how long a trip it is. I've had my fill of sailing."

I said I was in a house, that I did not drive, and I was about to add that I knew someone who might take them, thinking Keith and I would do it if he was able to borrow Unc's car or my family's station wagon — and if he wanted to make the drive. But before I could speak, the men threw more questions at me.

"Where is your house?" one of them demanded. "How far?"

"Three quarters of a mile, more or less," I said.

"Which way?"

I pointed, feeling uncomfortable. I didn't like his tone or the manner in which the dark-haired man was looking at me, sliding his eyes from my face down to my feet . . . slowly. I was glad it was cool enough for me to be wearing jeans and a sweater instead of a bathing suit.

"How far is the nearest house in the other direction?" he asked.

When I said it also was three-quarters of a mile, he uttered a curse, anger showing in his face.

The dark-haired man laughed coarsely. "Be thankful for small favors, Jim," he said. "It's not storming and you've got a groovy girl to look at. Even if we're minus food and whiskey, some of the good stuff is dry in the waterproof pouch. Why don't we enjoy what's available?"

He smiled at me and came closer. Almost in a reflex movement, I stepped away, seeing his face darken in annoyance. "You don't like me?" he asked. His eyes were glittery and what I'd first thought was a grin seemed more of a leer. "We have plenty of pot. You like grass?"

My mouth went dry. I shook my head, wondering if the strange glow in his eyes came from drugs. The thought had not entered my mind before; now it was frightening.

He grinned again. "You want something stronger?" he asked. "I think we can handle that request. Let's look over the supply and find out what we have that will appeal — "

"I have to go!" I interrupted him, my voice thin.

He jumped in front of me, blocking my path. When I tried to go to the side, he grabbed my wrists, his fingers like iron.

"Hey, baby. You hang around. Jim and I will show you a good time. Right?" He brought his face very near mine.

The question was superfluous. He was not asking me. His tone amounted to an order and I had no choice. I tried to twist from him but he tightened his fingers on my wrists until my hands were numb.

"You're hurting me!" I gasped. "Let me go!"

"Yeah, let her loose." The man called Jim laughed. "Let her loose — and send her over here."

I was shoved forward. Suddenly and hard. Jim reached out for me, his hands pinning my arms to my sides so that I was trapped in his grasp. A scream rose to my throat but it didn't come out. Screaming for help would be futile since nobody was in hearing distance. The men knew it too. Stupidly, I'd made that plain when I said we were three-fourths of a mile from either house.

"Take your hands off of me!" I gritted the

words out in a voice choked with terror. "Leave me alone!"

"Take your hands off of her right now!" The voice came from the top of Big 'Un. It was Dad, coming over the dune at a run.

I could not believe it! In my whole life I'd never been so glad to see anyone.

At that instant a dog barked. *Pit!* I would have recognized his bark anywhere.

Everything happened at once. Keith and Pit hurtled through the air and the man holding me loosened his grip so that I broke free just as Pit, the dog who never snapped or snarled, lunged at the stranger in the windbreaker, the dog leaping high, his teeth bared as he clutched the man's shoulder. The jacket material ripped but the dog did not open his mouth even though the man was slapping at Pit's nose.

"Get this damn dog off of me!" he hissed. "Call him off!"

I fled to Dad. He was panting from the run, his face flushed. "Jenny, are you all right?" he asked in a strained voice.

"Yes. They just wouldn't let me go."

"We weren't harming her! This dog — "

"Pit, come here," Keith said.

With his upper lip pulled back so that his teeth resembled fangs, the dog hesitated. The windbreaker was in shreds but there was no blood showing on the man's skin, so I assumed Pit's teeth had not penetrated the flesh. Finally, the dog obeyed and went to Keith.

Dad put his arms around me and my terror began to subside. If I had not been so shocked and upset I might have wondered what he was doing on the beach at sunrise so far from the cottage, but at the moment I was too shaken to question anything.

"I don't know who you are or what you're after," Keith said to the two men, "but you head out of here on the double and don't come back. You can be arrested for holding a girl against her will and this is private property and posted so you also can be charged with trespassing. If you don't leave," he paused, drawing a choppy breath, "Jenny will get the sheriff and I'll give my dog the command to go for your throats. Mr. West and I can take on one of you but the other one sure will be a mess with a chunk of his neck gone."

The strangers exchanged sullen glances and started to the boat, their backs rigid with anger. The terrifying thought that they had a gun in the waterproof pouch made me tremble, although apparently it was a needless fear on my part. They dragged the boat across the beach to the Sound, wading out as they pushed it until they were in deep enough water to climb aboard.

I turned to Dad — and caught my breath. His features had settled again into their familiar mask, and while his eyes didn't seem quite as expressionless as they'd been all summer, the rage he'd showed when he found the man holding me had disappeared.

"Dad — ?" My voice broke.

He turned. I almost said, "Are you all right?" but didn't, and was thankful to catch myself in time before the question was spoken. Instead, I asked how he happened to be on the beach so early in the morning.

"I heard a door close and got up to investigate. You weren't in your bed or in the cottage, Jenny, and I had an idea you'd be on the beach. I must have walked further than I realized." He moved his hand across his forehead, his eyes clouding again. "I'll go back," he went on. "Kay will worry if she's up."

He strode off, his hands in the pockets of his trousers, his shoulders hunched up as if he was walking against a stiff wind, even though the breeze was faint and the sun was warming the air.

"Your dad seems different," Keith said when my father was out of hearing. "I don't know what it is, but he's not the same."

"I'm aware of it too. Even his walking this far is a change. When he yelled and came over the dune, he looked as if he could take those men apart, but as soon as he saw I was all right, he seemed to slip back into his shell. If you hadn't told the men to go I don't think Dad would have been able to do it."

"Maybe the fact that you were in danger jarred him. Jarred his state of mind, I mean. Look at Pit. Did you see how he grabbed that guy? I've never known him to attack anybody before. He hates cats and won't even growl at them, but he really tackled that so-and-so. When I called him, I didn't know if he'd come to me or not. He could sense danger and was protecting you the same as your dad was, I guess."

As if he knew we were discussing him, Pit trotted up and rubbed against my legs. I knelt on the sand, stroking the dog's head.

Keith's attention was on the sailboat, which was growing smaller on the horizon. A sail had been hoisted. We could no longer make out the shape of the two men, just dark specks in the boat.

"Jenny, what happened?" Keith asked. "You're sure they didn't do anything to you? Didn't hurt you?"

"They scared me. I've never been so frightened. They offered me marijuana and claimed they had something stronger. I said no and it made them angry — they were already irked because I wasn't carrying food and didn't have a car parked nearby. They seemed to think it was fun to push me around as if they were playing some kind of a game. I was so thankful when Dad and you and Pit appeared."

"What were they doing here?"

"They said they were vacationing on the Outer Banks and were sailing yesterday when the storm caught them. The wind and waves were so high they couldn't control the boat."

"It's a miracle that boat didn't break up in the storm. Jenny, what were you doing out here this time of the morning?"

"Coming to find you. To say I'm sorry about yesterday."

"*You're* sorry?" his eyebrows went up. "It was my fault. What do you have to be sorry about?"

"For getting so furious — " I tried to smile and it came out all twisted. "And for not having a sense of humor."

"I'm the one who needs to apologize. It was rotten of me to let you dig. It seemed funny at the time, but — well, it's not so funny now and I don't blame you for being mad as the devil."

"Yesterday is over, Keith. Let's forget it. I will if you will."

"Okay," he grinned. "That's a true treaty and all treaties have to be sealed with something. We don't have any paper and ink on us but a kiss would be all right by me."

Smiling at him, I lifted my face to his. It was a very, very sweet kiss.

"Aren't you earlier than usual today?" I asked when I could get my breath. "I didn't think you'd begin jogging until six."

"I was coming to see you. I intended standing under your window and calling to you or whistling until you were awake so I could apologize. I'd have seen you last night in spite of the storm if we hadn't had a crisis at the house. Aunt Cammie broke her glasses and she can't see a thing without them. Unc was lying down with a headache when it happened and I couldn't walk out — not even for you. This really bears out what Jake told me about my coming here for the summer, that Unc and Aunt Cammie need a younger person with them."

"I wanted to come to you last night," I said softly. "But Dad and Kay refused to let me leave home."

"Thank goodness for that, as much as I'd have liked to see you. What if you'd been on the beach alone last night and those goons in the sailboat had found you? Especially if they were hopped up on drugs. You can't wander around away from the cottage after dark. Maybe it'll be a hundred years before another boat is beached here, but please don't run the risk. I couldn't take it if you were hurt, Jenny."

"You sound just like Dad and Kay with your instructions," I told him and smiled. The night before the orders for me to remain at the cottage were infuriating. Now, it seemed rather nice to have Keith worrying about me.

"I'm driving Unc and Aunt Cammie to their home town today and they want to be on the highway by seven o'clock, which is why I'm up earlier than normal," he said. "I started to drive to your place, but am I glad I didn't! If I had, I'd have been on the road instead of on the beach and I wouldn't have known you needed help. But I figured Pit and I could use a little exercise if we're to be cooped up riding for three hours." He looked at his watch.

"It's nearly six now. I'll see you home and hurry on back."

"You don't have to come with me. Nothing can happen now and I'm not afraid."

"Maybe I want to come."

I slipped my hand in his and we started for the cottage, not talking much at first. Keith's fingers were warm on mine, and he held them tight.

"What was that about your commanding Pit to go for the men's throats?" I asked.

"Pure bluff and blarney. They fell for it, though."

"Dad couldn't have helped if there had been a fight. It wouldn't have been that way before his accident, but now . . ." I let the sentence die. "Know what?" I said. "I'd planned to invite you to breakfast today. I was going to make you a bacon and cheese omelet. Muffins too."

"Give me a rain check. Don't forget, either."

As if I could, I thought.

Aloud, I said, "What time will you be back tonight?"

"It will take luck for us to come back to the beach by day after tomorrow, Jenny. Aunt Cammie put in a long distance call to her eye doctor and he'll see her as soon as we get there, but her glasses are complicated and the last time it took two days to get the lens made."

Two days. That seemed forever. I gave a small sigh that Keith heard and his hand tightened on mine.

"You won't be alone long," he said. "From the day I come back here to the end of the summer, I'll stick so tight you'll get fed up with me."

"Don't count on my being fed up. It'll never happen."

"I hope it won't, Jenny."

The cottage was in sight. Keith kissed me and I stood by the dune to watch him go, shading my eyes with one hand against the dazzling sunrise. He began to run, moving along the firm sand while Pit occasionally strayed to splash in the water. Twice Keith turned and waved, and I didn't go indoors until I could no longer see him or the dog.

CHAPTER 11

By the time I reached the kitchen, Dad had told Kay about the two strangers on the beach but apparently he hadn't gone into detail and she was full of questions. I related the incident, seeing her eyes widen as I mentioned Dad yelling to the men.

"Ed didn't say a thing about that," she answered. "He seems withdrawn now but at least he talked to me when he came in and it's encouraging to think he could go into action in an emergency. Maybe he's finally starting to come out of himself a little. Maybe . . . Jenny," she put her hand on my arm, "you're being truthful when you say that you're not hurt?"

"I'm fine. Honest."

At breakfast Kay asked if Keith and I had made peace, immediately smiling and answering her own question.

"You don't have to tell me, Jenny," she added. "It shows in your face."

Time dragged without Keith. Remembering the first week at the beach, I wondered how I managed to endure those seven days. Now I only had two or three days to kill before we'd be together again and each one was hopelessly long.

After a solitary swim in the morning, I spent most of the first afternoon napping to make up for my lack of sleep the previous night. At dusk I went down to the beach again, sitting on the sand in front of the cottage to watch the sunset colors fade and the sky turn a dark irridescent blue. "Good night, Keith," I whispered as the stars came out, and I returned to the cottage to read until bedtime.

The next day was similar, but the third day of Keith's absence was very different. It was, as Kay later described it, "the day that changed our lives."

That morning I was on the porch, moving restlessly from the swing to a chair, going back to the swing, not conscious that Dad was aware of my fidgeting. I was thinking about Keith and wondering if he missed me, fearing that maybe he'd seen a girl he had known from years of visits to the Coopers or that perhaps he'd met a new girl, someone prettier than I was. More attractive. Sexier.

Kay came to the porch to ask if either Dad or I wanted any items from Clayton's Store.

"Toothpaste," I told her.

"Let's tag along, Jenny," my father said. "You seem to need a change of pace."

I was so astonished that it took me a moment to respond. My eyes met Kay's and a huge smile was spreading across her mouth.

"Yes, do come. Both of you," she urged.

It was the first time my father had been in an automobile since the June day Mr. Hunter drove us from the airport to the cottage. I had ridden to Clayton's Store a couple of times with Keith when he was buying groceries for Aunt Cammie, and while I could not classify the country store as a hubbub of excitement, in my mood that morning I'd have gone anyplace.

When we arrived, Dad decided to wait in the station wagon. I went into the store with Kay and as soon as we were out of Dad's hearing, we clutched each other's hands. "Can you believe it?" she beamed. "He *is* going to get well! I know it! I can see improvement every day!"

"Do you think he'll be completely well by the time we go home?" I asked.

"We'll have to wait — and hope. But if he makes as much progress in the next month as he has in the past few days, I should imagine he'll want to go to his office when we reach Cincinnati. He can try a couple of hours a day at first and gradually extend the time. That'll also mean he can pick up the rest of his life. Isn't it a miracle!"

"We won't be at the beach another full month," I reminded her.

The first of September I'll be telling Keith good-bye, I added to myself.

During the return ride to the cottage I mulled over the conversation with Kay. Dad not only talked more of late, but he was eating better. Most of the time his face showed some animation and he had lost the gauntness, which made him seem old and ill when we left Cincinnati. The psychiatrist must have been correct. Time, quietness, and our understanding and support were healing my father.

I closed my eyes, remembering how it used to be with Dad joking and laughing, planning things for Kay and me to do. It would be wonderful to have a real father again instead of this shadow of a man, to be able to go to him, to share the closeness we'd once had.

The day was such a scorcher I decided to stay out of the sun until late afternoon. Following lunch, my restlessness returned, and just to be doing something, I took one of the jigsaw puzzles from the living-room bookcase, set up a card table on the porch, and got to work. The picture on the puzzle box showed a garden scene with flowers of every color.

Kay was in the kitchen making a blueberry pie, and Dad, sprawled on the swing, eyed me and offered advice.

"You're going about that the hard way, Jenny," he commented. "Why don't you take care of the border first? Then you can fill in the rest."

"That's the scientific approach and you

know how un-scientific I am." I grinned. "Sorting through all the puzzle pieces to separate the ones with straight sides is a bore."

He did not reply. Glancing at him, I saw the interest on his face. "How about giving me some help?" I said. "You do the border and I'll tackle the ones with red flowers on them."

He surprised me by pulling a straight chair to the far side of the card table and in no time the border took shape. Dad was fitting pieces together faster than I did.

"I haven't tried a jigsaw in years," he said. "Not since before Charlotte died. She used to enjoy doing them, especially on a rainy weekend."

My stomach heaved. I could not remember when Dad last spoke my mother's name, and he had just said, "Charlotte," in a casual tone of voice.

"Do you still blame yourself for Mom's death?" I blurted out. Instantly, I was shocked at myself. The question was in my mind but I never meant to utter it aloud.

"I blame myself for lots of things, Jenny-girl," he murmured sadly.

"Dad, you mustn't! You just mustn't!" I ran to him and threw my arms around him. "When you blame yourself for something that's over you might as well be alone on a mountain top, because you're shutting me out! Shutting Kay out too! Dad, we need you and it's breaking Kay's heart for you to build a wall about yourself and not let her in. Or me, either. I want everything like it used to be with all of us laughing and having fun. I want to be able to come to you when I have problems and to tell you if everything is wrong at school. You've always helped me, but now, when you're wrapped up in yourself, I don't know if I matter to you or not! And I don't want it that way. I love you and I need you and — oh, Dad — "

The words tumbled out and I could not stop them. Fear choked me, fear that what I'd said to my father would be more than he could bear just when he was beginning to be himself again. My tirade might push him back into his shell of self-damaging silence.

But the opposite appeared to be happening. I forced myself to look at him. Something different showed in his eyes, an awakening, a new consciousness. I dared not move. At last, he gave a faint smile and reached under my hair to tweak my ear, a gesture he used to make when I was a little girl.

"Dad, I'm sorry," I moaned. "I didn't mean to — to speak that way."

"It's all right. It's all right."

He pushed his chair away from the card table and stood up. I caught my breath. My heart was beating twice as fast as usual.

"Thank you, Jenny-girl," he said softly. "I'll help you finish the puzzle later."

He went into his bedroom and closed the door. Kay was in the kitchen and from where I sat I could see her back. A strange suffocating sensation swept over me. I needed to be alone. Completely alone. I had to get my tangled thoughts and emotions under control.

I went outside and walked along the water's edge. Pamlico Sound was as blue as the sky, the water dappled with a golden sheen from the afternoon sunshine. Strolling aimlessly with my mind on Dad, I didn't realize I was heading toward the Coopers' until Big 'Un came into view. I was near the spot where the two men beached their sailboat and despite the hot sun on my shoulders, I shivered.

If Keith had been at the Cooper house, I would have gone there, but I turned at Big 'Un and retraced my path to the cottage. *Keith* . . . I thought, aching to see him. I gazed out at the Sound, wondering if my feeling for Keith was real love, if he and I were truly in love or if we had been drawn together because of circumstances, because both of us were lonely and isolated from other teenagers.

No matter how he felt about it, I knew my emotion was genuine. As deeply as I cared about Dad and Kay— and about Mom — I'd never known the kind of all-engulfing affection for anyone that I had for Keith.

In less than four weeks he would be returning to Milwaukee for the winter and I'd be going back to Cincinnati. An acid taste came into my mouth at the realization of how short a time remained for us.

All of a sudden I hated autumn, which had always been one of my favorite seasons. Now

I dreaded it. A tremendous lump rose into my throat. Nothing could ever be the same for me when Keith was one place and I was somewhere else. I would miss talking and laughing with him, kissing him, feeling the warmth of his hand on mine and his arm around me.

If only this was June, I sighed . . . and the summer was just beginning.

CHAPTER 12

We had dinner on the screened porch that Friday evening, the August days noticeably shorter with the mellow twilight closing in soon after the sun went down. Kay put a tall white candle under a hurricane globe in the center of the table, the glass protecting the flame from the wind. She and Dad talked more during the meal and several times I realized he was looking at her with the sort of glance they used to exchange when they were first married. Kay had to be aware of it; there was a sparkle in her eyes and a softness about her mouth.

For the most part I remained quiet. I was thinking of Keith and at the same time remembering my outburst to Dad. If they noticed my silence, it was not apparent.

Kay's blueberry pie was delicious. "Plenty of pie is left, Jenny," she said. "You and Keith can finish it up for a snack tonight."

"It's so late now I doubt if he will get to the beach before tomorrow," I replied, trying not to show my disappointment. All day I'd hoped and waited, and at the moment it was hard to reconcile myself to another evening without Keith.

As I began clearing the table, Kay followed me into the kitchen with a tray of dirty dishes.

"Jenny, Ed seems different tonight. He talked twice as much as usual and a little while ago he came in the kitchen and nuzzled his chin against my hair like he used to do. I just couldn't believe it at first." She was speaking too softly for Dad, who was on the porch, to hear. "I wanted to stop you when you spoke so bluntly to him while both of you were working on the jigsaw puzzle, but maybe you were right to do it."

"I surprised myself," I confessed. "Scared myself too. It could have been the wrong thing to do."

"I don't think it was. I suppose the time was right for Ed to be given that kind of straight-to-the-point statement. I would never have dared do it, not when your mother was involved. Before this last accident that wasn't the case, but these past several weeks — months — I've been careful to avoid referring to Charlotte or to any incident that might bring painful memories back to Ed."

"You actually started Dad getting well, Kay. You brought him here."

"I only followed the doctor's orders."

"Last May I thought the whole deal was a

nutty scheme and hated to give up the swimming pool job." My face burned at the recollection of how uncooperative I'd been. "I guess I tried to put my judgment ahead of yours and the psychiatrist's, which wasn't smart of me, but last spring I didn't see how a place like this would do much for Dad."

"You'll never know how many doubts I've fought," she sighed. "The months of May and June were nightmares. Thank God all those weeks are behind us and today makes the rough times more than worthwhile. For Ed to help you when you were in trouble is the most encouraging sign of all, and then tonight . . . I don't know how to express it, but he seems more normal, more like himself."

She gave me a swift hug and started from the kitchen, pausing to add, "Do you mind finishing by yourself, Jenny? It's such a lovely night I think I'll see if Ed would like to go outside."

After assuring Kay I'd be glad to tidy up, I put the dishes in hot suds for a brief soak, then went to the porch to crumb the table and blow out the candle. It was amazing how much light came from the one small flame. When it was gone, the porch was awash in misty blue haze.

Dad and Kay were on the beach in front of the cottage, holding hands, their bodies outlined against the Sound. They did not need me or see me. It was too private a moment for a third person. Dad might not be fully well, but he was on the way. I was positive of it.

A few early stars shone vividly in the turquoise sky. A familiar lump came into my throat. It was partly relief that my father was so much better, but along with that emotion was wistfulness caused by my being alone, a feeling I knew would linger until Keith returned.

As I dried the last dish, the yellow beam of a car's headlights cut into the darkness from the road at the rear of the cottage. I saw it through the kitchen window, dropped my towel, and hurried to the back door, hearing Pit's whooping bark.

"Keith!" My voice rang out.

The motor died and the automobile lights went off. I raced down the cottage steps. Keith was already coming toward me, Pit at his side.

"What are you going to do first?" Keith asked in a teasing voice. "Pat our four-legged friend — or kiss me? Both of us are eager for greetings."

I laughed from sheer happiness. "Pit's awfully cute, but — " I began in the same tone he'd used.

The sentence was never finished. It was impossible to talk with Keith's mouth on mine and his arms around me.

Some minutes later he told me his news. Jake was at the Cooper house.

"Jake telephoned last night from New York," Keith explained. "He'd just landed at LaGuardia and he tried calling the beach but didn't get an answer so he put in a call to Unc's home phone and found us. All the flights south were booked until this morning so he spent last night in New York. Aunt Cammie's new glasses weren't ready until noon today and after we got them there was an extra sixty miles to the airport to meet Jake before we could head for the beach, which is why we're this late."

"You're here now." I was all smiles. "That's what counts."

"I dropped the others off at the house and came straight to see you, Jenny. I can't wait for you and Jake to get to know one another."

"When can I meet him? Tonight?"

"Tomorrow. The jet lag has gotten to him and he said he was going to turn in early." Keith swallowed a yawn. "I'm bushed, too. Sorry not to stay with you longer, but it's been a full day and I was so excited about Jake's arriving that I couldn't get to sleep until late last night. Besides, I hate not to be at the house on his first evening."

Keith kissed me again before getting into the car. "See you in the morning, Jenny," he said, turning on the ignition. As if to add, "Me too," Pit yelped.

I did not want Keith to leave. "Wouldn't you like a slice of blueberry pie? Kay made it and — "

I spoke too late, my voice lost in the noise of the car's engine. The tail lights fast became tiny red specks down the road.

A strange little prickle of fear started at the base of my backbone and crept upward. *I am not jealous*, I told myself. *I am not!* It was absurd to consider being jealous of a boy's relationship with his father.

Still, the troubled sensation persisted in me. I leaned against the railing of the back steps and stared disconsolately across the sand into the trees. The tall pines swayed in the night wind. There was something eerie about those silent trees . . . or maybe the fear tugging at me provided the eeriness.

Keith had been waiting the entire summer for Jake's return. With so little time remaining before September, he would want to spend a big part of each day with his father — and who could blame him? But that meant Keith's and my lazily happy hours of swimming, playing games, building sand castles, talking, all of it intermingled with loving kisses, were over. Now, Jake would be with us. Or, Keith constantly would eye his watch so he could rejoin his father.

Either way, I would lose.

CHAPTER 13

The resemblance between Jake and Keith was so strong it gave me a jolt. Jake was heavier but both had the same tall, lanky builds, the same quick smiles. Keith's light-brown hair was streaked gold by the summer sunshine as was his father's, and each possessed a square jaw and intensely blue eyes.

I was prepared to be polite to Jake but not warm, an attitude which let me know I actually was jealous no matter how I tried to deny it to myself. However, when I met Keith's father it was impossible not to like him. There was an open friendliness about him, a natural sincerity, which drew me as a magnet would have done. Thinking about it, I realized this was the identical appealing trait I'd noticed in Keith that first June morning.

On the morning after his arrival, Jake came

114

to our cottage with Keith and talked to Dad and Kay as well as to me. Dad seemed at ease, obviously enjoying the visit and conversation. They discussed Jake's trip in detail and when Greek architecture was mentioned, my father's face glowed with interest. Apparently Jake had a good bit of knowledge about building, and the talk became technical, laced with architectural terms.

After a time Keith and I left the others on the porch and took a swim. Pamlico Sound was as smooth as a lake. We waded out waist-deep and flattened our bodies on the surface of the water, matching our swim strokes until Keith yelled, "Far enough, Jenny," the signal to head toward shore again. I rolled over on my back and floated, allowing the current to carry me in, my eyes shut against the blinding sun.

"How do you like Jake?" Keith asked.

"Lots."

It was good to be able to reply honestly although I expect I'd have lied and said I liked Jake whether I did or not.

"You mean it, Jenny? That's great!"

Treading water, Keith stayed beside me. "Jake likes you," he went on. "I could tell. Ditto for how he reacted to your folks. My father can be very, very silent when he doesn't care much for the people around him, but he's gabbing with your dad and Kay a mile a minute right now. It's almost as if they were old friends."

Still floating, I moved my head to look at Keith and blinked water out of my eyes. "How does Jake plan to keep himself occupied the rest of the summer?" I said. "While he's here, I mean. I — uh — I guess you and he will be off by yourselves most of the time, won't you?"

The words did not seem quite as I'd intended. Embarrassed, I began to swim, pulling ahead of Keith. He caught up with me in a hurry with some long strokes.

"What are you trying to say, Jenny?" he asked.

Without replying, I continued to swim until I could touch bottom. Both of us stood and I dug my toes into the wet sand under the water, wishing I'd kept silent about my fears. There was no adequate explanation unless I told Keith the truth, which I did not want to do, and with his steady gaze on me, I felt flustered, unable to come up with any sort of logical answer. He must have sensed my uneasiness because he reached for my hand and curled his damp fingers through mine.

"If you're scared you and I won't have any time to ourselves, forget it," he said softly. "Honestly, I'm not going to let that happen and you don't have to worry. Anyhow, Jake probably will thank you for keeping me out of his hair."

Without looking at Keith, I gave a jerky shrug. "Don't make idiotic assumptions," I muttered.

"It's a fact, Jenny. Jake has a big cardboard box of notes he made when he was in Greece and he wants to get them organized and typed up while the memory of the trip is fresh. He brought his typewriter here to the beach and at breakfast this morning he said he planned to put himself on a work schedule. Until he has those notes in order, he can't use the information in teaching the ancient history classes he'll have this fall."

A weight seemed to lift from me. I practically danced through the water to dry land and the smile I gave Keith was as bright as the reflection of the sun on Pamlico Sound.

CHAPTER 14

The supper party a week later was Kay's idea and, amazingly enough, Dad seemed excited at the prospect of having guests. It was another indication that he was getting well.

"The Coopers have been such good friends to us I want to invite them over for a meal," Kay said. "That includes Jake and Keith, of course."

"And Pit, who probably would show up whether he was included or not." Dad grinned at her. Then he looked toward me. "Does this meet with your approval, Jenny-girl?"

"You know it does," I answered.

Anything would have suited me so long as it involved Keith. My fears about seeing little of him now that Jake was back had proved to be silly.

Kay planned Dad's favorite hot weather menu for the supper: a chicken and rice casserole, crunchy with toasted almonds, broccoli, fresh fruit salad, and what my father had always called "the best lemon meringue pie on the continent." Dad and I helped with the food preparations and Keith pitched in on the party morning by joining me in dicing chicken.

The change in Dad was spectacular. He no longer sat in one spot and stared blankly. Now he seemed to want to be busy and he helped Kay around the cottage as well as going with her each time she headed for Clayton's Store. His interest in the party was spontaneous, while a short time earlier he would have been repelled at the thought of guests coming for a meal.

"Kay, you're a whale of a good cook," Keith commented as he selected another chunk of chicken and cut it into small cubes. "Everything I've ever eaten that you made has been super."

"Only reason I married her," Dad said with mock seriousness. "That and the fact that she's beautiful and talented."

Keith and I laughed, continuing to chop the meat. Dad offered to make watermelon and cantaloupe balls to go in the salad if he could find an implement to work with, and Kay quickly put a tiny melon scoop in his hand with the statement that she would not turn down any offers of assistance.

"But don't nibble! I know you," she added. "You'll eat your way right through the cantaloupes if my back is turned and there won't be enough fruit left for tonight."

Dad immediately popped a melon ball into his mouth and grinned.

Things seemed to be becoming normal with my family, Dad joking and talking, all of us laughing together. My father still had moments of despair over the two tragic automobile accidents, but he was learning to control his emotions and to live with his painful memories.

Keith went home in the middle of the afternoon and returned at dusk driving Aunt Cammie, Unc, and Jake. Pit came too, the dog the first out of the car. Freshly bathed and shaved with his blue slacks and shirt making his eyes seem bluer than ever, I thought Keith had never looked more handsome.

The party was perfect. We sat around the porch table, everyone praising Kay's food, Unc, Jake, and Dad swapping funny stories about places they'd been and things they had done. In the candlelight Kay was especially lovely in a sheer white dress, and Aunt Cammie's eyes glowed behind her thick glasses, the soft light hiding the wrinkles in her worn skin until she appeared much younger than her almost-eighty years.

I felt Keith looking at me and when I glanced toward him he stared at me with an admiring expression in his eyes. Maybe in the candlelight I'm beautiful too, I mused. Whether I truly was or not, if he thought it, that was fine.

Following dessert, Aune Cammie asked if anybody wanted to have a bridge game. Jake begged off, but Kay's face lit up.

"I'd love it," Kay answered and turned hopefully to Dad, who nodded. I did not believe he would have wanted to play ten days earlier.

"Ed and I used to play bridge often," Kay remarked. "We're one of the rare married couples who can play as partners without getting into a fuss."

"We're not," Unc chuckled. "Cammie's a tiger when she sits at a card table, so you team up with her, Kay. Ed and I will form a united male front against you women."

"I'm not going to be a witness to whatever happens," Jake said laughingly. "Jenny . . . Keith, how about you non-bridge players coming outside with me?"

CHAPTER 15

Keith, Jake, and I settled ourselves on beach blankets near the water. A gentle breeze blew off Pamlico Sound and the quarter moon made a luminous arc in the sky. Pit put his head in my lap and went to sleep. It seemed natural for Keith's arm to slide around my waist and I leaned against his shoulder, content just to be near him. Occasionally laughter drifted to us from the porch where the bridge game was in progress. For a time we didn't feel the need to talk.

Jake finally broke the silence. "Peaceful here, isn't it?" he asked quietly. "It's hard to realize people are hurrying on highways and rushing about in cities, or that at the resort beaches there's a lot of frenzy with music that's too loud and the air smelling like stale french fries. This is so serene and beautiful it's the way everything must have appeared when the first settlers came ashore."

"Unless," Keith said in a flip tone, "before they landed, they were attacked by pirates. I never should have said that. If you mention pirates when you're with Jenny she goes into orbit. That's a fighting word to her."

"Keith — really!" I exploded. "You're exaggerating!"

"What's he talking about, Jenny?" Jake asked.

I drew a long breath. "It's not *mentioning* pirates that sends me into orbit, to borrow your phrase." I made a face at Keith. "It's the people — one person especially — " I stared at him again — "who let other people dig for buried treasures, under false pretenses and on a scalding hot day, no less. Okay, Keith! You brought up this subject so you tell your dad about the dirty trick you pulled on me!"

Keith grinned, his teeth very white in the misty dark. "Thanks, but no thanks."

"You're scared," I teased.

"This is your chance for revenge, Jenny. Your version of it may be slightly different from mine."

"One of you open up," Jake cut in. "You're causing my curiosity to work overtime."

I made a big thing out of how I had believed some long dead pirate placed the fourteen rocks in a straight line pointing to the spot where valuables had been hidden. I described my frantic digging before making the discovery that I was the butt of Keith's hoax, and I didn't leave out a detail.

Jake smiled before the story was half finished and as I wound up with a dramatic, "The End," he turned to Keith. "What sort of guy are you to do a dumb thing like that?"

"A dumb one," Keith muttered. Jake and I laughed.

"Right." Jake shook his head, but he was smiling. "It's a miracle Jenny didn't tell you to get lost for keeps."

"I was awfully mad at first," I admitted.

"I don't blame you for that. You've forgiven me, though. Haven't you?" Keith pressed his cheek against mine as he spoke.

"Yes, you're forgiven," I said. "I can laugh about it now. Laugh at myself. Not a big horse laugh like you probably give when you think about the episode, Keith. But a small laugh."

Pit stirred in his sleep, changing position. My mind was still on the pirates.

"I wish I'd come across something interesting at the end of the line of rocks that day — and not merely to show Keith up," I said. "Jake, Keith told me you don't think pirates buried what they stole. But do you suppose there's a chance . . . even a small chance . . . that you're wrong? That something valuable might be hidden near here?"

"I've been wrong before." Jake's voice was thick. "Many times and about many matters. In Greece this summer, for instance. The four of us on that dig who have graduate degrees had studied ancient documents and maps, not to mention cross-checking references as to the possible location of towns no longer in the historic writings. Yet — " he flung his hands out, palms open, "we came up empty. Very frustrating, I assure you."

"Jake, did you honestly expect to find a buried town?"

"I certainly did. So did the others."

"That's a shame," I murmured.

"I believe we were on the right track," Jake added, "but our time and money gave out before we had any success. Perhaps the next group investigating that particular site will be able to go down deeper and get better results."

We became silent again. My mind was on the pirates. Maybe, I thought, my disappointment wouldn't have been so keen if I hadn't genuinely been interested in the history of the area. I didn't merely want to get rich by discovering a buried chest — although I wouldn't have objected to coming across something valuable — but I'd hoped to have the thrill of being really close to a part of the American history I'd read about.

In front of us the black waves seemed to be growing larger, spewing out white foam as they broke several yards from shore, the water slithering to land and ebbing away. A wispy cloud passed across the moon.

"Jenny, what did you hope to find when you were digging?" Jake asked.

"I didn't think I'd unearth a sea chest full of gold or diamonds, but I'd have been happy over any small item. One coin . . . or a rusty spoon. Anything. It sounds corny, but I wouldn't even have minded too much coming across an *empty* box or chest in the ground, although that would have meant someone else got to the treasure before I did."

"You aren't making sense," Keith cut in. "Who wants an empty box?"

"Finding an empty box would have been proof that this is historic soil. I've never been to a historic place that wasn't protected by guards and loaded with tourists and so covered with posters and arrows telling you what to see next that you lost the feeling of being where something important had happened once. I guess if I'd come up with an empty chest, even if I didn't find any valuables, it would have convinced me that pirates actually came here."

"No question about pirates being in and out of this area in the early 1700's," Jake replied.

I gave him a hard look. "Do you mean I might be sitting this very minute where Blackbeard once sat — or stood or came ashore?"

"Could be." Jake smiled. "If not Blackbeard, some other pirate famous during the first part of the eighteenth century. He may have set up a base here while he careened his ship. There's a sloping beach here now but this coastline changes constantly, and when Edward Teach was alive — Teach is Blackbeard's legal name so far as we know — this may have been a deep-water cove. Teach considered Pamlico Sound and the Pamlico River his personal waterways."

My interest rose. "What others, Jake? Blackbeard is the only pirate whose name I'm familiar with."

"Stede Bonnet was in this area quite a bit. He was known as the 'gentleman pirate' since he was a retired British army officer of the King's Guards before he turned to stealing. He owned a big sugar plantation on the island of Barbados and apparently wasn't in bad need of money, but some of the people who knew him thought he went to sea to get away from his nagging wife."

Keith and I laughed softly. Jake stretched out full length on the beach blanket, his arms under his head.

"John Rackham was another pirate who hung around here," Jake continued. " 'Calico Jack' Rackham. He got the nickname because his clothes always were made of calico cloth. Jenny, do you know there were women pirates in the early 1700's? They were plenty tough. Dressed like men, which was unheard of at the time, and fought like men."

I had not known it and was eager to hear more. Jake mentioned Anne Bonney and Mary Read, adding that Mary's activities were more or less veiled except for her death.

"Anne was the illegitimate daughter of a lawyer in Ireland, and the story goes that Anne's mother was a maid in the lawyer's house. The scandal of her pregnancy caused the man to lose his law practice and he came to the Colonies, bringing the maid, who passed as his wife, and the child. Anne married a chap named James Bonney who was a pardoned pirate. Then, she fell in love with 'Calico Jack' and left her husband to go to sea with Rackham. Mary Read was a crew member on Rackham's ship at the time and both women were captured along with the men pirates and condemned to hang after a trial before a Court of Admiralty in Jamaica."

I caught my breath. "So they were executed," I said.

"No, they weren't, Jenny. They told the judge they were pregnant — and they were. 'We plead our bellies, M'Lord,' they're supposed to have said in court. Neither of them went to the gallows although Rackham and the men were hanged."

"What happened to them, Jake?"

"Mary died in prison of a fever and Anne was held in prison on the island of Jamaica until her child was born. Afterward, she was given reprieves from time to time but there's no record of her execution. She — "

He stopped abruptly and groaned.

"Why haven't you two shut me up?" Jake's voice was rough. "I didn't mean to rattle on as if I was teaching a class in history and that's what I've done. Guess I got into one of my favorite topics and I didn't know when to quit."

"Please don't stop," I begged and meant it. "I want to know about Blackbeard. Was he as bloodthirsty as stories about him claim? Did he really build a house on the Pamlico River near where we are and have lots of wives?"

"No question about his being a character," Jake replied. "There aren't any records of his having murdered or maimed his captives *if* they submitted to his authority. When he took a vessel, if everyone on board did what he ordered and did it quickly, the crew and the passengers didn't need fear for anything except the loss of their property. If somebody resisted, though — watch out! Let one person refuse to take off a diamond ring and Teach would chop it off, finger and all."

Shock and dismay put a tightness in my throat.

"As for his wives, he had thirteen or fourteen of them — so-called wives. When he'd reach port, if he took a fancy to a particular girl, he'd arrange for his first mate to perform a marriage ceremony, which apparently was to make the girl think she was his legal wife. When he tired of her or was ready to go, he'd give her a few gifts and put her back on shore."

"I don't see why anybody would want to marry him," Keith said.

"He must have had a certain charm because when he decided to settle on land and moved to Bath some months before his death, the townspeople apparently didn't object enough to force him out."

"Maybe they were scared of him," Keith said.

"That's possible. He was a walking arsenal with knives and pistols stuck into his belt along with a three-foot long cutlass which he'd had especially made and which hung at his side. He had some education as he left correspondence and log books. He's bound to have presented quite an appearance with the weapons and the fancy clothes he liked. Long coats made out of rich fabric. He would plait his beard and tie ribbons on the pigtails."

I stared into the darkness. As far as I could look in an eastward direction there was nothing except water and sky, but my imagination let me see a pirate ship on the distant horizon, her white sails billowing out in the wind with the skull and crossbones flag flying from her mast. For a few minutes I'd been caught up in the color of swashbuckling legends without remembering how awful it must have been to be aboard a ship captured by ruthless pirates.

We became silent once more. The tide was coming in, long swells of water reaching higher and higher on land. Jake held his arm up so he could see his watch.

"It's nearly midnight," he said, getting to his feet and brushing sand from his trousers. "You two are good listeners and I've bent your ears long enough for one evening. If the bridge game hasn't ended, let's see that it does. We should be heading home."

I was stunned to realize I had forgotten about Dad and Kay and the bridge game, about everything except the pirates.

With my hand tucked into Keith's, we started up the dune to the cottage, moonlight spilling over us. My mind lingered on the fascinating tales I'd just heard about Calico Jack and Anne Bonney, about Blackbeard. Jake had made them seem like real flesh-and-blood human beings, not merely names on the pages of a history book.

CHAPTER 16

Halfway into our final week at the cottage the lovely sunshine was replaced with a storm warning.

"I hope it's not going to be a hurricane," I said to Keith.

He and I were out of doors, but instead of wearing bathing suits, we had on jeans and heavy sweaters. The air was chilly and Pamlico Sound was a mass of frothing whitecaps under a dark-gray sky. It was hard to remember that only twenty-four hours earlier we were swimming in calm blue water and complaining about the ninety-nine-degree heat.

"Don't worry about hurricanes, Jenny," Keith said. "They used to descend without any advance warning, but now the weather bureau doesn't let that kind of storm creep up. We would have had a message to evacuate if a hurricane was on its way. The Coast

Guard has maps showing the location of every house, trailer park, and camp ground in this area and we'd have been told to leave the beach and go inland."

"Hurricanes go inland too. Sometimes weathermen make mistakes . . ."

"You are in a glum mood." He grinned and put his arm lightly around my shoulders. "Quit borrowing trouble. We'll get a storm and probably it will be a bad one, but I'm not expecting a hurricane. Want to play Monopoly? That'll get your mind off the weather."

I said yes and we went to the cottage. As I was taking the game board from its box, an automobile horn blew, a noise I had not heard since we left Cincinnati. It startled Keith as much as it did me and we ran to the back window.

Our station wagon was pulling up near the pine trees. Kay drove with Dad beside her on the front seat.

"Jenny, is Keith with you?" Kay called.

"Yes," Keith answered.

"I'll give you a ride home, Keith," she said. "We stopped at the Coopers' a few minutes ago on our way here from Clayton's Store and your Aunt Cammie is very anxious for you to be home before the storm breaks. She's had the radio on all morning and apparently we're in for a bad piece of weather. She doesn't want you walking near the water if there's lightning and that makes sense."

"What did I tell you?" I gave Keith a triumphant stare. "It might be terrible."

"Aunt Cammie goes bananas if she sees one square inch of gray in the sky."

"I wish you could stay here," I added wistfully.

"I'll go now to make her happy — and come back as soon as it fairs off to make you happy. 'Bye for now."

When they returned from the Coopers', Dad stopped under the cottage for an armful of firewood. The dry logs caught quickly, warming the room. We had lunch by the hearth, commenting that hot soup was especially good on a damp, bleak day.

By four o'clock in the afternoon it was as dark outside as twilight. If I had not broken my transistor some days earlier, we could have listened to weather reports and maybe I wouldn't have felt isolated, but it seemed to me that we were completely cut off from the rest of the world. Dad and Kay began a game of backgammon; I tried to read, but could not concentrate, wishing desperately that Keith was with me.

Storm noises filled my ears. Waves boomed and intermittent thunder rolled in the distance. The storm was getting nearer and the wind's howl was fearsome.

I won't worry, I repeated to myself, attempting to rationalize that since the rain had not started, the black clouds might blow away. But I made the mistake of going to the living-room window and an uneasy quiver shot through me.

Water was higher on the beach than any tides since we came to North Carolina. Wind gusts swirled dry sand from the tops of the dunes and as I watched, the zinc-colored sky blazed yellow with a jagged streak of lightning. I froze, waiting for the thunder. It came in a series of crashing thuds. Our lights flickered and went off, leaving the room gray except for the red coals in the fireplace.

"We'd better round up all the candles and flashlights," Dad said. "The electricity probably will be on shortly, but we'll be prepared. I'll get more wood although I don't want to make a big enough fire to send sparks up the chimney, not in this gale."

"Ed, maybe we should leave here," Kay ventured, her voice laced with apprehension.

Footsteps clattered on our back stoop before Dad could reply. I opened the door, letting Keith and Jake in, both of them wearing waterproof parkas with handkerchiefs tied across their noses and mouths. Each carried an armload of short planks.

"I think you folks should get over to Unc's," Jake suggested. "They don't have any electricity, either, but if the tide keeps on rising, you could be marooned since this cottage is on a point of land jutting out into the Sound with water on three sides. It will be safer at Unc's with his house set back in a cove and more sheltered. Keith and I will board up the windows and — "

"You're going to stay here?" I interrupted, my eyes on Keith. I did not want him marooned any more that I wanted it to happen to myself.

"Only long enough to get everything shored up," he said.

Dad offered to help, but Jake refused. "It's familiar to Keith and me as we've done it before and we don't have to nail the barricades up. When Unc built these two cottages he had metal brackets installed outside the windows. Once the shutters are hooked, we can slip the planks over them into the brackets."

"Is this a hurricane?" Kay asked the question. I was wondering also.

"It doesn't have an 'eye' at the center so, technically, it's not classified as a hurricane although the winds are strong enough for it to be," Jake explained. "According to the last radio report two storms are converging on Pamlico Sound at the same time, one coming up from the south and the other moving in from the northeast, which means we'll catch it from several directions. Now, let's get into action. We can talk later. Each of you take a change of clothes in case you get wet and whatever toilet articles you'll need overnight. And hurry! Driving is rough and it will be worse once the rain starts. Put the station wagon in the shed when you reach Unc's.

There's room for it and if you leave a car out in this wind, the glass could be pockmarked by blowing sand."

Keith, following his father to the door, paused. "Tie a scarf over your face, Jenny," he said. "That sand really stings when it hits your skin."

Dad must have taken Jake's orders to heart because he kept urging Kay and me to hurry, and in ten minutes we were ready to leave the cottage. I didn't realize how savage the wind actually was until we inched our way to the station wagon which was parked beyond the pines. The trees dipped and swayed, the branches crackling as they meshed together. Bits of broken twigs torn off by the wind sailed through the air.

My head was ducked but sand peppered my cheeks through the scarf and my eyes burned. Dad, walking between Kay and me, held our arms and I had the feeling my feet would have been lifted off the ground if he had not clutched me tightly.

I carried a small overnight bag with clothes for us, and Kay had two cartons of milk. She'd grabbed up the first items she saw in the refrigerator, knowing it was a senseless gesture.

"I hope I can drive in this weather," she mumbled. "If the wind takes the car off the road — " She seemed to be talking as much to herself as to us.

"I'll drive," Dad came back.

"Ed," she said softly, "you haven't touched a steering wheel since spring!"

I had the same reaction, every nerve in my body pulled taut. Kay had not said "since the accident," but that's what she meant.

"I'm not a better driver than you are, Kay, but I'm a more experienced one," Dad came back. "Let me drive."

It was a relief to get into the car. If Dad felt fear about the automobile, it did not show. Kay was as pale as a ghost, but my father exuded confidence. I wondered what was going on in his mind, if being in the driver's seat made him remember the details of the last accident or if sensing Kay's uneasiness he only wanted to help her. If that was true, he was much, much better. Maybe he was well.

Dad turned on the ignition and the tires spun, but we did not move. He mashed hard on the accelerator until the station wagon lurched forward and we crept down the narrow road at ten miles an hour, the car rocking while the windshield wipers struggled futilely to keep sand from caking. We rode in silence. All of us were deep in our own thoughts.

Unc and Aunt Cammie were waiting for us and an hour later, Keith and Jake arrived just as the rain began to fall. The storm intensified, thunder rumbling constantly above the noise of the wind and rain, but with the house shutters closed we did not see every zigzag of lightning. Two kerosene lanterns provided light, and a log fire made the Coopers' living room cozy.

"How long does this type of storm usually last?" Kay asked Unc.

"Brace yourself for a couple of days although I hope we'll be lucky and the time will be shorter. Don't be afraid that the house will blow away with you in it because the contractor who built this place — and your cottage — was raised on the Outer Banks and he knew about weather in this area. He put the pilings down very deep and anchored the roof extra tight."

"All my life I've heard and read about storms off the coast of North Carolina," Dad said. "From what I'm seeing today, I can understand why this shoreline is so changeable."

"Yes," Unc's tone was crisp. "The wind and water make adjustments in the landscape to suit themselves. Even Ocracoke Inlet isn't in the exact spot where it was a few centuries ago. Hurricanes did that."

"Stop discussing the weather!" Aunt Cammie ordered. "All of us will feel better after we eat, and it's going to be a cook-it-yourself meal."

We roasted hot dogs over the fireplace coals and after we ate, Aunt Cammie brought out her banjo. Everybody sang. When one song ended, somebody promptly started another as if our music would drown out part of the storm. Keith and I sat on the floor and held hands, our backs braced against the wall.

At bedtime, Aunt Cammie took charge. "It's my house so I'm making sleeping assignments," she announced. "Jonathan and I are old enough to stake a claim on our bed whether we have guests or not so we'll be in our room. Kay and Jenny will take the other bedroom, and you men," she looked at Dad, Keith, and Jake, "can camp out in the living room. We have sleeping bags as well as plenty of pillows and blankets."

I missed Keith's good night embrace, but was glad he didn't kiss or hug me in front of our families. It seemed too private a thing to share. He gave my hand a special squeeze and we smiled at each other.

"You owe me a kiss," he whispered. "I'll collect it tomorrow — or as soon as we're alone."

"I'll remember," I said softly.

The room Kay and I shared was where Keith and Jake usually slept. We had a flashlight but undressed in the dark to save the batteries, and as I crawled into one of the twin beds, a particularly loud blast of thunder reverberated through the house.

"I didn't realize how tired I am until I got into a horizontal position," Kay said, yawning.

"Me too. But I'm not sure I can go to sleep. The storm is so noisy it makes me jittery."

"I know, but concentrate on relaxing. Think

about something pleasant instead of the weather. Good night, Jenny."

I murmured, "Good night," and pulled the covers to my chin, closing my eyes as I tried to ignore the rattling shutters in the boarded-up windows and the heavy drumbeat of rain pounding the house.

Think about something pleasant, Kay had advised. I thought about Keith, about the pleasure we had just being together, about the way his eyes always smiled before his mouth did, and about the sweet-salty taste of his lips when he kissed me. He was, I decided drowsily, the pleasantest thing I knew.

CHAPTER 17

When I opened my eyes I was aware of the silence, not complete quiet, but the normal morning noises of seagulls squawking and footsteps in another part of the house. A faint edge of light seeped under the window shutters and the glow-in-the-dark clock opposite the bed showed the time, seventeen minutes past nine. It took a few seconds for me to grasp that this was morning and I had slept more then ten hours.

The others were in the living room and the shutters on the windows there were open with patches of blue sky showing behind the billowing gray clouds. Pamlico Sound was choppy although the violent waves of the previous evening had subsided.

"Hey, look who finally came alive," Keith grinned.

"I must be the Number One sleepy head," I murmured.

"Each of us straggled out at a different time, Jenny," Aunt Cammie told me. "We don't have any electricity yet, but I have a kettle of hot water on the hearth for instant coffee or tea and there's plenty of bread, butter, and jam."

Dad and Kay, who were ready to leave for the cottage, offered to wait until I'd had breakfast. Jake was accompanying them to take the boards off the windows.

"How about walking with me, Jenny?" Keith cut in. "Jake wants me to come by way of the beach to check out any storm damage there."

It was easy to say yes. In three days we would be going home and I did not want to miss a moment with Keith in the small time remaining.

I returned to the bedroom for my sweater, and Kay followed me.

"Jenny, he's changed, isn't he?" she asked.

"Yes. Definitely! Yesterday I was frightened when he said he'd drive us here. But. . . ."

"I don't believe it was an easy decision for him because I saw the set to his chin when he turned on the ignition. But he did it. That's the important part. He made himself do that because he knew I was nervous about driving."

"Do you think it means he's stopped being afraid of cars?" I asked.

"I hope so. If he's still frightened, at least he's able to cope with the fear." She looked at me with a twisted smile. "I hope it's more than that, Jenny. I hope he's enough himself now to realize how much you and I need him. He responded to you on the beach when those two men had you and he realized you were in danger, and yesterday — well, he was a part of the family again and that's how I want things to be. Everything will be all right — I can feel it in my bones."

"Kay, are you ready?" Dad called her from the living room.

Her smile widened. She squeezed my arm as she left to join him.

The outside air was cool with a fresh breeze blowing. The bits of blue in the sky grew larger.

"When did the storm end?" I asked Keith as we left the Cooper house. "I slept so hard I didn't hear anything."

"Neither did I. Jake said the rain started slackening off around three o'clock this morning and stopped at daybreak. From the looks of everything, we might get sunshine later on. I hope so."

We followed the shoreline, and after a slight curve, which put us out of sight of the house, Keith stopped walking and caught my hand, bringing me to a halt before turning me so that I faced him.

"Seems to me that last night I remember telling you that you owed me something," he said mischievously. "I can't quite think what it might be."

"Oh, you can't?" I teased. "I guess I must have forgotten too."

"Have you?" He laughed and drew me into his arms, becoming serious as he kissed me firmly on the mouth. "That was for good night last night," he said softly. "This is for now . . ."

The second kiss was tender and lingering. When it ended, neither of us spoke.

We resumed walking, Keith's arm around my shoulders and mine about his waist. I felt happy and at peace. Keith and I were together. Dad was so much better he was practically well. The storm was severe but none of us were hurt by it.

After a while I said, "The beach looks different and I can't figure out why."

"I was thinking the same thing, Jenny. Maybe it's because the tides were so high yesterday that this strip of packed sand is broader than we're accustomed to seeing. Hey — " His eyes widened. "Jenny, Big 'Un is gone! Look at that twisted bush way over inland! That's even with where Big 'Un should begin and the dunes running parallel with the Sound seem to be like they've always been! But Big 'Un just isn't here!"

"You must be mistaken! A mountain of sand that large can't vanish."

"You think not? It can. Didn't you see how the wind was blowing sand yesterday? If the rain had begun early the sand would have been wet and less likely to blow, but that didn't happen. These dunes and sandbars and shoals are forever shifting. That bush — the twisted one — is the landmark and I know this is the spot where Big 'Un should be."

"Keith, you don't suppose the cottage . . . The wind . . ." My voice broke and I could not make myself say aloud that the cottage might be gone despite Unc's assurance that it was well built.

"Let's hurry, Jenny!"

He walked so fast I could not keep up without dog trotting. Finally, we ran.

As we came near the cottage both of us stopped. My first reaction was relief that the house was standing, but immediately I saw the unbelievable changes around it.

The big dune which sheltered one end of the screened porch had been flattened until it was only half as tall as before, and while the cottage looked to be intact, water now reached much nearer the front steps. Part of our wide beach had been sliced off.

"Look *under* the cottage," Keith commanded gruffly.

I did, holding my breath. The cottage now seemed to be situated on a knoll with the pilings and shed hidden by a bank of sand. We were unable to see through or walk under the house as we'd done all summer, and the shed and stack of firewood were buried as if they never existed.

"Let's check the back." His tone was grim. "Who knows what the situation is there."

On any other morning if we wanted to go

to the back we'd have walked under the cottage. Now, we circled it, both of us stunned as we rounded the building.

"The rocks! Where are those fourteen rocks?" I gasped.

Not one of the rocks was visible. Every speck of pine straw had vanished and in its place was an expanse of white sand reaching from the back stoop into the trees, mounding to make a higher elevation than we'd had formerly. Some of the pines had been blown down and lay at weird angles pointing in every direction. Other trees had broken limbs.

"Keith, do you suppose the wind picked up the rocks, one by one?" I asked in an unbelieving voice.

"I don't know. After what we've just seen, I suppose anything is possible. Maybe the rocks are still where they were but are covered with sand."

I started forward toward the trees — and stumped my toe. Reeling, I teetered, flinging both arms out to keep my balance.

"Are you all right?" Keith asked.

"Yes. What did I trip over? I don't see anything."

But I had felt something. I dropped to my knees to investigate, expecting to uncover one of the fourteen rocks now moved from its former resting place.

It wasn't a rock, but a brick. The reddish tan brick lay a few inches below the surface. I tried to pick it up and could not budge it.

"What in the world — " Keith stooped by

me. He also tried to take the brick out and failed. Both of us started digging with our hands.

"I've got a brick!" he shouted. "And it's attached to something! Look — here's another one — "

"Do you think we've found a pirate vault?" My voice was thin with excitement. "A safe to hold valuables?"

For once, Keith did not contradict me. I sucked my breath in. He was as convinced as I was, the expression on his face a study in absolute concentration as he scooped sand and tossed it aside.

"We need a shovel!" I jumped to my feet — and remembered that the tools were in the shed and there was no way we could reach the shed door.

"A shovel is what we should *not* use, Jenny," he came back. "Jake told me that when an archaeologist finds a buried object he uses spoons and his fingers. A shovel might hit what's hidden and smash it. Whatever we've found seems to be built in a curve. I'm going for Jake!"

He dashed to the cottage. I was still on my knees, digging, when he returned with Jake, Dad, and Kay.

"What is it?" I asked. "A pirate hide-away for valuables?"

"I don't know," Jake answered. "These bricks definitely are in an arc and they didn't fall into that arrangement, not with mortar between them. Let's see the rest of it."

Everybody pitched in. I paid no attention to the time but at least three hours must have gone by before the full circle of bricks was uncovered, some of them crumbling but the shape intact. The ring was hollow, about five feet in diameter and measuring some two feet in height. The center held a pile of sand.

"These bricks were put down by a trained mason," Dad commented.

"How can you tell?" I asked.

"It takes a pro to do that good a job of forming a curve with rectangular objects. See how evenly they're lined up with more mortar toward the outside of the circle and less toward the inside? The bricks are laid in English bond."

"What's 'bond'?" Keith inquired. I did not know, either.

"The bond is the arrangement of the bricks, the pattern," Dad explained.

"English bond was popular in the late seventeenth and early eighteenth centuries," Jake said. "There's a chance this structure — whatever it is — dates back to that time."

To Blackbeard's era. A surge of exhilaration shot through me.

I didn't care about the details of construction, just its purpose. "What was it used for?" I persisted.

"I'd say it was a kiln," Dad answered and Jake nodded in agreement.

"You mean it's only an oven?" My eyes went from one of the men to the other. "The kind of kiln where potters bake dishes?"

"Could be," Jake replied. "Perhaps potters used it or the kiln might have had another purpose."

"Of all the rotten luck . . ." Disappointment washed over me. A kiln was anything but exciting. It wasn't even interesting, much less glamorous.

"You're positive this wasn't a vault built by pirates for holding their treasures?" I asked, unwilling to give up a dream.

"It doesn't appear to be a vault, Jenny-girl," Dad said. "It's too small for a house or even a room, and with the top finished off, it was hardly a foundation or a cellar. Nobody builds round chimneys on buildings. The inside of the circle is enough darker than the outside to indicate it was once used for fire, and a kiln would be the logical explanation."

I choked down a sigh. What had started out to be a marvelous discovery was nothing, and I turned away to hide my dejection. All I had to show for my efforts was a tired back and ten broken fingernails.

There is no explanation for what I did next. It wasn't planned — it just happened. Standing up, I stretched to get the kinks out of my shoulder muscles and, on impulse, took a flying leap into the sand-filled center of the brick circle. If I thought at all, I must have anticipated a soft landing. Instead, my foot struck a hard object and I gave a surprised, "Oh!"

Dad extended his hands to help me out. I

wasn't really hurt although one foot tingled.

"This sure is your day for stepping on strange things, Jenny," Keith said. "What did you hit this time?"

He crawled into the center and carefully plunged his fingers through the sand, bringing out an uneven lump of shiny, black, glassy substance about the size of a grapefruit. Dad took it, examining the strange glob. Continuing to sift sand in the middle of the circle, Keith located half a dozen smaller lumps of the same glistening black substance.

"That's tar!" Dad exclaimed.

"You're right, Ed!" Jake turned the largest piece over and over. "This must have been a tar 'kettle,' a brick oven used to cook pine rosin to make tar for caulking ships."

"How can we find out who built it?" Keith asked.

"I doubt if we can," Jake answered thoughtfully. "Courthouse records would show the name of the owner of this land two or three hundred years ago, but that doesn't necessarily mean the property owner set foot here. A sailing ship captain could have ordered it built if his vessel had been grounded in heavy weather and he needed tar for repairs."

"A storm like the one we've just had or a hurricane must have covered it with sand and that's what preserved it," Dad said. "Buried away from air and moisture, the tar didn't rot."

Jake smiled in my direction. "Jenny, you

have your pirate treasure, I believe. Perhaps 'Calico Jack' Rackham brought his ships here for fresh caulking on the seams. Or, it might have been Blackbeard."

I was hardly thrilled. "Not much of a treasure," I mumbled, the letdown catching up with me. "If only we'd found something beautiful . . . and valuable. Anything but plain old tar."

"Don't sell it short. You don't know it, but you've made a historical discovery as valuable in its way as a sea chest of jewelry would have been," Jake went on. "The kettle and tar bits aren't as pretty as rubies and gold bars, but this is an important find. I'm going to notify the State Historical Commission and the archaeologists they send out will be ecstatic."

I kept quiet. My hopes had been built up while we were digging, which made the disillusionment even worse. The disappointment hurt like a physical pain.

"You may not feel pleased about the tar kettle, Jenny, but I am," Jake said. "It's made my summer because this means I've been on one dig that netted something important. That helps to make up for not locating anything in Greece."

The sincerity in Jake's voice touched me. He meant every word he was saying and the excitement in his eyes was obvious.

Keith was watching me and I glanced at him. There was a softness in his gaze. He understood my feelings. He knew how much I wanted to find a pirate chest.

Jake's enthusiasm was greater than mine because I'd much rather have come across something glamorous, but, I reflected, Jake had a point about the discovery. At least Keith and I had found *something*.

CHAPTER 18

After breakfast the next morning while Kay and I were making beds she told me Dad wanted her to cancel our plane reservations for Cincinnati.

"He wants us to drive home in the station wagon," she continued happily. "Wants to get off the superhighways and drive through some of the small towns. Not stop and visit the buildings, but to see the exteriors. 'Quaint American Gothic' is the term he used to describe some of the older houses and churches in this part of eastern Carolina."

"Kay, that means he's thinking about architecture again."

"I know. It's a sign to me that he's ready to go back to work."

"Do you think he'll help with the driving?"

"He offered to do it. Said he realized I'd be exhausted if I drove the entire trip."

I caught my breath at the realization of what this meant. "Dad is himself. I know he is!"

"I think so too. He's warm and loving, just the way he was before the accident. It's as if . . . as if he'd been closed up inside a musty attic or cellar all these months . . ."

"And finally came out," I finished for her.

On the final day Keith and I scarcely had a minute to ourselves until after supper. There was a good-bye visit to the Coopers, and Jake joined us for a last swim. We helped Dad and Kay pack, clean the cottage, and load the station wagon for an early start the next morning.

At sunset Keith spread a blanket on the sand and we sat at the edge of the water as we'd done so many other evenings, only this time there wasn't any laughter or silly conversation. The sun was half over the horizon, a huge, red-orange ball which sent golden streaks shimmering over the surface of Pamlico Sound.

"When will you and Jake go home?" I asked.

"In about a week. The archaeologists from the Historical Commission are due here day after tomorrow to see the tar kettle and Jake doesn't want to miss them. After that we'll move Unc and Aunt Cammie inland and we'll head for Pennsylvania. I'll be there a couple of days with him and go on to Wisconsin."

A tremendous lump came into my throat. I had so much to say and couldn't find the right words. Suddenly, I was afraid I was going to cry.

"Know something?" My voice was shaky. "I didn't want to come here, and now I don't want to leave."

He put his arm around my shoulders. "It was like that for me too, Jenny."

"I was rotten to Kay when she told me I didn't have any choice about spending the summer in North Carolina with her and Dad, and the first week we were here I thought I'd die of loneliness. But you came and — oh, Keith, it's been the best summer of my entire life! The very best!"

"It turned out to be great for me and I didn't want to come, either. I'd never have showed up if it hadn't meant a lot to Jake to know Unc and Aunt Cammie weren't by themselves." He gave a soft laugh and nuzzled my hair with his cheek. "I guess that's what my Mom calls 'following the dictates of your conscience.' Mom is a nut about consciences. She claims you can never find any honest-to-goodness happiness unless you quit thinking about yourself all the time and think about other people, too."

It was true, I decided. Doing something for Dad resulted in wonderful happiness for me. Kay had not wanted to leave her job in Cincinnati, but she did it for my father and now she was radiant. When Dad stopped dwelling totally on his own misery and thought about what his depression was doing to his family, he felt better.

The sun dropped out of sight, the corals and lavenders of the sunset fading as the sky darkened into a rich blue. A sprinkling of stars began to show and the gentle waves on Pamlico Sound eased to shore with the barest trace of murmuring.

"Keith, I'll die if I don't see you until next summer!" I blurted out.

"Hey — quit worrying. You couldn't lose me if you tried."

"But — "

"Milwaukee is not that far from Cincinnati, Jenny. Lots of holidays are coming up. I might be able to see you over Thanksgiving and for a couple of days during the Christmas vacation and — "

"And New Year's and Valentine's Day and the Ides of March and Income Tax Day and — and whatever else we can find," I broke in, giggling.

Laughter eased the moment for us. I became serious again.

"Keith, it won't be the same next summer, even if both of us come back here . . . will it? Dad has told Unc we'd like to rent the cottage again, but . . . but I guess you and I will change during the winter. We'll be older . . ."

"Sure, we'll change. Everybody changes all the time. But that doesn't mean we'll stop caring about each other or that we won't continue to have fun together." He tightened his arm around me, his voice tremulous enough for me to know his emotions were as deep as mine. "You're right about next summer not being identical to this one, Jenny. But I'm counting on it being even better — and that's saying a lot!"

It was a promise to carry us through the winter. Keith put two fingers under my chin and tilted my face up to his. His kiss was warm and loving and I put my arms around him to return it.